THE RISE & FALL OF THE GALLIVANTERS

THE RISE & FALL OF THE GALLIVANTERS

A NOVEL BY

M. J. BEAUFRAND

AMULET BOOKS NEW YORK

Library of Congress Cataloging-in-Publication Data
Beaufrand, M. J.
The Rise and Fall of the Gallivanters / M. J. Beaufrand.
pages cm
ISBN 978-1-4197-1495-5 (hardcover : alk. paper)
[1. Friendship—Fiction. 2. Punk rock music—Fiction.
3. Bands (Music)—Fiction. 4. Missing children—Fiction.
5. Family problems—Fiction. 6. Sick—Fiction.] I. Title.
PZ7.B3805782Bel 2015
[Fic]—dc23
2014013556

Text copyright © 2015 M. J. Beaufrand
Title page photograph copyright © 2015 Getty Images
Book design by Maria T. Middleton

Printed and bound in U.S.A.
10 9 8 7 6 5 4 3 2 1

Amulet Books are available at special discounts when purchased in quantity for premiums and promotions as well as fundraising or educational use. Special editions can also be created to specification. For details, contact specialsales@abramsbooks.com or the address below.

ABRAMS
THE ART OF BOOKS SINCE 1949

115 West 18th Street
New York, NY 10011
www.abramsbooks.com

FOR BILLY RANCHER

ON THE LAST DAY OF SEVENTH GRADE, our drama teacher, Mr. Piper, decided to make us play Mafia. It was one of those wasted days that happen at the end of every school year. We'd finished our work, our grades had been sent to our parents, and we were all hopped up on cake and vacation.

Normally we liked Mr. Piper, even though he wore Jesus sandals in the middle of winter so the middle school auditorium always smelled like foot fungus. He used to preach about Movement, which meant us bouncing off the walls while he played bongos. "That's it!" he would tell us. "*Be the snowflake!*"

But that last day of class, in a weird turnabout, when our brains were already in Johnson Creek, or Cannon Beach, or just Out of Here, Mr. Piper decided to impose classroom structure on us in the form of Mafia.

If you haven't played before, it may sound cool, but it's actually kind of stupid. Everyone has to lie down on the floor in a circle and close their eyes. Then the teacher taps someone to be the hit man and someone to be the angel. He says, "Mafia, awake!" Then the hit man sits up and opens his eyes, and points to the person they want to kill. That's all they do. Sit up and point. And boom! The guy's dead.

Ah, but there's redemption. The hit man lies back down, then the teacher says, "Angel, awake! Who do you want to save?" Then *they* sit up and open their eyes, and if they point to the same person the hit man pointed to, then the victim gets to live. The hit man and angel keep going until everyone is dead. In between hits, when everyone has their eyes closed, Mr. Piper will announce which of us has been "saved" and which of us has been "killed," so everyone can try to figure out who the angel and the hit man are. Then the real fun begins. Everyone tries to imagine how they died.

None of us had actually watched someone's life drip away, or be shot away, so it was more about drowning in vats of lemon Jell-O, or being trampled in a herd of stampeding nutrias.

I didn't realize until later how freaky it was that everyone wanted to die.

Dying was the fun part.

I was the first one to get the tap. I didn't even need to

ask if I was the angel or the hit man. I knew. Even then I had a reputation.

When Mr. Piper said, "Mafia, awake!" I pointed my finger across the circle of kids lying around, some smart-asses with their arms crossed over their chests like cadavers. I cocked my finger like a gun straight at Crock, who even then was kind of obnoxious. Then I lay back down.

After that it was someone else's turn. I heard Mr. Piper say, "Angel, awake! Who do you want to save?"

As I lay back with my eyes closed, someone else sat up and tried to undo my damage.

My turn again. Again and again I sat up and pointed. Again and again someone tried to save everyone else.

There were thirty kids in the class. Number twenty-seven I pointed to was Jaime, and number twenty-eight was Sonia. I didn't even point to the one Mr. Piper had chosen as the angel, because I knew without looking who it was.

When the bell for the end of class rang, everyone sat up and opened their eyes. Well? they wondered. They didn't need to ask who the hit man was. But the question was, when do we get to guess how everyone died?

Mr. Piper gaped at me, and at my best friend, Evan. No one had ever gotten three for three, let alone twenty-six for twenty-eight. "It's uncanny," he said. "You two must share some kind of cosmic connection." The only two we'd mixed up, it seemed, were Sonia Krajicek and Jaime Deleuze.

Ev and I talked it through on the bus home—not about the ones we'd gotten right, but the ones we'd gotten wrong. Evan thought Jaime was the last one I'd want to kill because (a) she was the first girl in our class to develop a rack (and believe me, it was a good one), and (b) he didn't think she could handle being dead. He was right about that. She was always running off crying to the bathroom because some boy had teased her about her hair or her clothes, when really they only wanted a grope. Yeah, try explaining that to a twelve-year-old girl. It's not about you. It's about your boobs.

But I countered with Sonia: Had Ev seen the way she moved, those legs sprouting up long and sexy? The way she flicked her black hair over her shoulders when she was studying her algebra book? The way she'd look at me with those soft brown eyes when she told me to fuck off? No, Sonia was the cool one. Sonia was the last one I'd ever kill.

That was years ago, before Ev had his appendix out. Before my father left, and then came back. Before we became the Gallivanters. Before Ziggy entered our lives suddenly and deserted us just as quick.

After everything was over, and only three of the four of us walked away, I kept remembering that day in seventh grade, and realized that Ev and I had been asking each other the wrong questions. It wasn't, who would we want to save *last*? It was, who would we want to save *at all*?

Every day since, I've wished that Mr. Piper had chosen me for something else.

Now, every night before I go to sleep, I feel a tap on my shoulder. But this time my role is different. He doesn't call me *hit man*. He whispers, "Angel, awake! Who do you want to save?"

This time I know what I have to do to make things right. Night after night, I try to call him back. Night after night, I shake the blankets off, sit up, and point.

"NO, NOAH. ALIENS DID NOT EAT YOUR GREMLIN."

It was two o'clock in the morning and we couldn't find my beloved car, Ginny the Gremlin, pale blue on the outside with a burgundy and brown herringbone interior. Getting behind the wheel was like biting into something that looked chalky and boring, like Maalox, and discovering it gushed sweetness, like chocolate and cherries.

It was just Ev, Crock, and me. We'd been kicked out of the Satyricon a whole hour before and had spent our time threading the downtown streets trying to find my car. Finally I threw up my hands and said that maybe aliens had eaten her. Because that was the only explanation. It was 1984 and everyone knew an alien invasion would happen at any time, and that when they overran us, they would be wearing silver jumpsuits, permed hair, and jungle-cat eye shadow.

Crock and Ev and I joked about it all the time, but right now Ev didn't think it was so funny. And who could blame him? We were stranded and out of ideas, and by the looks of it he had another migraine coming on.

He was leaning against a beige brick wall of the PfefferBrau Haus, his rainbow dreads falling around his shoulders. His face was scrunched tight and he was pinching his nose. He used to say he could feel those headaches before they hit, they were like a halo of pain. That was when he was supposed to catch it, when it was just a halo. Not later, when his head felt like someone had pinched it in a vise and screwed it up tight.

I had to get him out of there soon.

We really needed my car.

The only thing we could agree on was that we'd parked it next to a dumpster by the PfefferBrau Haus, but here was the problem: The PfefferBrau Haus took up multiple city blocks, and the brewery wasn't exactly square. It had alleys. It had grain chutes. It had skybridges. It had railroad tracks (railroad tracks!) with no trains. It had multiple corners with multiple dumpsters, and that nasty smell like someone was cooking cereal in tomato soup.

"Let's circle around one more time. Maybe we left it on the other side of the brewery."

"Please don't say 'brew,'" Crock contributed from the curb, where he was unhelpfully sitting, head between his knees, waiting for Ev and me to solve the problem of how we were going to get twelve miles home to Gresham.

I hated Crock so much at that moment. Bad enough that, thanks to a passable fake ID, he'd been in the bar shotgunning microbrews, leaving Ev and me stranded in the mosh pit, and that he borrowed my "I Have Seen the Abyss and Went to Denny's" button without asking and was wearing it now, flecked with spew.

But honestly: Couldn't he have made an effort? As it was, that drunk homeless guy in the tinfoil hat was more helpful. At least *he* had raised his head when we asked him about my Gremlin, and muttered something about monstrous evil lurking in the bowels of the city, blah blah blah. You know, the whole end-is-nigh crap.

"Maybe we're remembering the sign wrong. Maybe we left it in front of the plasma center?" Ev asked. His voice came out all wrong, like a grunt. We all donated plasma. It was like donating blood, only for cash. Not much cash, though. Just enough for the latest Ramones album.

I shook my head. There was no mistaking the Pfeffer-Brau Haus. And then there was its history. I'm not a superstitious guy, but the only reason I'd parked here was that no one else wanted to. It was as though what happened to Sherell Wexler was contagious, even though that's stupid. After all, you can't catch a case of having your throat slit and being shoved into a vat of porter, can you?

This place creeped all of us out. All the more reason to forget about the piece of paper in my pocket.

I slipped my hand in to make sure it was still there.

And it was. I knew without looking it was the color of beer froth and blood. I had the writing on it memorized, having folded it and unfolded it a million times in the club bathroom, to the beat of synthesizers and drum machines cranking out a rhythm that, whatever it was, wasn't music.

Ev bent over. He had a bad case of grow-out. Under the dreadlocks was a layer of baby-fine blond hair. They were impressive dreads, long and dyed all the colors of the rainbow. Our senior class at Gresham High had voted him Most Unique—a title I *clearly* deserved—just because he had better hair than any white guy living or dead.

He said, "Listen, I know how much you love your car, man—"

"Ginny. Her name is Ginny."

"—but I think we should call your sister. Just for tonight. We'll look for your car in the morning."

He was right. It was the middle of the night and we were stranded in the warehouse district of northwest Portland. The buses had stopped running hours ago. We didn't have enough cash for a cab to Gresham.

We were screwed.

That was when Ev's eyes squeezed shut in pain. He slammed the heels of his hands into his eye sockets and doubled over. You would think I would be used to that by now, since Ev's suffered from migraines since puberty, but I'd never seen him like this. He was writhing on the sidewalk, rolling right on the black spots of old gum and cigarette butts.

I rushed over to him and put a hand on his shoulder. "You okay, Ev? You pack your meds?"

"DOES IT LOOK LIKE I BROUGHT A PURSE?" he barked. "Shit!"

I remember thinking, *Oh god. This isn't a migraine. Something else is going on*—when *he* appeared, the guy who was about to change all our lives.

He came out of the brewery shadows, walking loose-limbed and easy.

The hair was what I noticed first. It was egg-yolk yellow and poufy and high. He looked in our direction without seeming to really see us. He was wearing a loose blue shirt under a yellow thousand-dollar jacket, and he exuded cool.

Could it be . . . ? He looked a lot like David Bowie. And we would know, because Ev won a look-alike contest that netted him a one-hundred-dollar gift certificate to Jojo's Records. This was years ago, in his pre-dread days, when all his hair was still blond and baby fine.

Behind me, Evan groaned. I propped him up against a wall, but he slid down it, his eyes practically rolling back into his brain.

And Crock? Crock still had his head between his knees. So I was the only one who saw the guy. And real thing or wannabe, he was here, he wasn't vomiting into a storm drain, and his eyes weren't yellow and unfocused, like the drunk in the tinfoil hat. We needed help and we needed it now.

I went right up to the guy in the thousand-dollar suit. Even his eyes were freaky and mismatched, like the real Bowie's. One of them was all pupil.

"Hey, mister," I said. "Can you help us out? My friend here is sick and we can't find my car. Have you seen it? It's a '78 Gremlin. Maalox colored."

Bowie casually lit a cigarette, crooked a finger that meant *Follow me*, and disappeared back into the shadows.

I still don't know why I followed him. What kind of idiot was I, following a strange man into a brewery where they brewed teenage girls? I could've been jumped. I could've gotten my throat cut, my punk ass cooked. Following that guy was dangerously stupid.

I knew all this, but Evan needed help. Without my car, I couldn't get him home.

I took my first step into the darkness. Then another. And another, sure I was about to bonk into a brick wall. But I didn't, because there was no wall where Bowie had disappeared. There was open air, a space wider than my arm span. It had been camouflaged in the shadows.

Two steps later, my whole body slammed into something huge and metallic that smelled like garbage and had a hollow ring to it.

Another dumpster.

I felt along its sides, and when it ended, my knees rammed into something just as metallic, only pointier. The grille of my car.

I pulled the keys out of my back pocket and felt my way to Ginny's driver's side, unlocking the door. The interior light came on, and there was the chocolate/cherry upholstery. I sank into it, running my hands along the dash. I may have kissed the steering wheel.

I was about to start the engine when there was a rap on my window. I jumped into the stratosphere.

Two great mismatched eyes were staring at me from under a cap of poufy yellow hair.

I cranked the window down.

"You need to get your mate some aspirin. The All-Nite Pantry on Burnside's still open."

I closed my eyes and listened to his voice. It was lyrical—even the English accent had overtones.

I wasn't a shaking-hands kind of guy, but I held out my hand anyway. "Thanks, mister . . . ?"

"You can call me Ziggy," he said, thrusting his own hands in his pockets. Apparently he wasn't the shaking-hands type either.

"Thanks, Ziggy. We were in a bad way." I started the engine.

See? I thought to myself. Nothing freaky about him. No hunting knife. Just a well-dressed look-alike who'd happened to save our asses.

And just as I convinced myself that everything was

normal, Ziggy said something that blew me into the stratosphere again.

"Oh, and Noah, you need to show them the flyer in your pocket. There's a darkness coming. I know you can feel it. Someone needs to make a stand, son. It has to be here. *It has to be you.*"

With that, he stood back, hitched up his collar, rapped twice on the roof of my car, strolled back into the shadows, and was gone.

THERE'S A DARKNESS COMING.

Duh.

As far as I was concerned, it was already here. Crock and Ev and I were eighteen years old, and all we did was lurch from darkness to darkness. The Satyricon. Johnny B Goode's. Hamburger Mary's. The kids with the skateboards in Pioneer Square who had no suburb to go home to.

Then there was the Disappearing Wall.

"I have seen the abyss," I mumbled as I parked in the Gresham Denny's parking lot. Denny's seemed to be the next logical step—at least according to my button that Crock was wearing.

It was three o'clock in the morning. I'd gotten Evan some aspirin at the All-Nite Pantry, and now he was lazily waking up from a comfortable snooze in the shotgun seat. Crock was in the back. He hadn't barfed since getting in the car, but I was still going to detail the backseat later.

Ev blinked when he saw where we were.

Normally he'd try to act cool when we went to the Gresham Denny's because my older sister Cilla worked there, slinging Grand Slam breakfasts to drunks and chain-smokers and truckers.

Cilla was three years older than us. At one point she wanted to be a beautician, but instead she was stuck here in Denny's, her skin slowly going yellow from secondhand smoke.

Evan didn't see her that way. To him, she was still the girl who'd babysat the two of us when we were nine and she was twelve. He never stopped trying to get her attention. First with his drawings of his favorite Trail Blazers superstars, then later, when he learned the first few chords of "Smoke on the Water," he tried to impress her with his musical genius.

Even now, when we were eighteen and she was twenty-one and he was clearly cooler than she was, he still thought of her as my glamorous sister who'd sat in his kitchen, talking on the phone to a long string of loser boyfriends, painting her nails some shade of ruby, and reapplying her Strawberry Lip-Smacking Potion.

Now, in my car, he said, "I thought we were going home, Noah."

But it was too late. He'd caught sight of my sister through the window and was already sitting straighter. He tucked his dreads into the collar of his army jacket. If he'd been in massive pain the hour before, you wouldn't know it now.

"There are things we need to discuss," I said.

The three of us walked into the breezeway and were assaulted by the smell of sugar and grease and stale pies and Marlboro Lights.

Ev and Crock walked ahead of me into the restaurant. I stopped to stare at the posters tacked to the corkboard above the bubble gum machine. The Disappearing Wall, Cilla called it. Which was stupid because the wall itself wasn't disappearing. It was what was *tacked* to the wall that was fading away.

This may not have been the pit of darkness Ziggy had talked about, but it was at least a satellite.

The giant corkboard was supposed to be a place for people to advertise mixed-breed puppies and lawn-mowing services. Lately, a different kind of poster had been taking over.

When I came in last week, there had been four of this new kind of poster. Tonight I counted ten.

The faces were all different, but the messages were the same: "Have you seen this girl?" "Last seen wearing . . ." "Reward for information."

Ev came back and stood by my shoulder. He didn't say anything, just read the Wall.

"Whoa. There are a lot more than last week."

I should've torn myself away, but I couldn't stop reading. There had to be some pattern, some quality to these girls that made them the same type. If there was, I couldn't find it. They were all teenagers, but that was it. There were blondes and Asian girls and black girls. They were tall and short, rich and poor. They were last seen on Burnside Street or Alameda Street or Vista Boulevard. They went to Wilson High. They went to Grant High. They were last seen wearing miniskirts. They were last seen wearing sweats. They were on their way home from a friend's house. They were on their way home from the library. Youth symphony. Volleyball practice. Saturday Academy.

The worst one by far was at the bottom left-hand corner. It didn't have a reward. It didn't have a phone number. Just the face of a girl with short brown hair, wearing a caption like a yearbook title that said only *Please.*

"Noah, don't stare at this too long, okay?" Evan said. "It'll only bring you down."

I agreed. "Idiot Willy says the parents are expanding their searches. They're getting more desperate."

Idiot Willy was Crock's stepdad. He was a cop. He and Crock didn't get along, but I couldn't always blame Idiot Willy for that.

Now Evan buried his hands in his pockets, slouched, and looked away. As he walked off, he mumbled something that I could've sworn sounded like "Aren't we all."

Cilla was behind the counter when Ev and Crock and I came traipsing in. She was holding a coffeepot that emitted a god-awful burned smell. Her hair was curled and her lipstick and eye shadow were so shiny and glossy they looked like a perfect layer of frost. But all that grooming couldn't take away from the fact that she was in a puke-colored zip-up dress with a grease stain on the collar and her name stitched on the front pocket. My sister's shift would be over in two hours, but in a lot of ways, it was never going to end.

"Shouldn't you be in bed, nimrod? Mom expected you an hour ago."

"We need a booth," I said, staring her down.

"Fine," she spat. "But I hope you've got money, because I'm not giving you any freebies. You can pay for your own goddamn pancakes."

At the lunch counter, half a dozen sad-sack truckers slouched a little farther in their stools. They hadn't done anything wrong, but Cilla had a way of making everyone feel like bad, bad dogs.

"Just coffee for us, thanks. Bottomless."

She snorted. "There's a surprise."

She showed us to a table with red Naugahyde benches, slapped down paper place mats showing pictures of platters of fake eggs garnished with orange slices and parsley, flashed us a smile just as papery and fake, and stalked off.

When she was gone, Crock said, "Seriously, man? Was there some reason we couldn't go straight home? I need my beauty rest."

Crock's shirt opened to show way too much chest hair. He thought he was studlier than Ev and me. I tried not to think about Crock's personal life too much. I mean, I liked the guy well enough, but he was a legacy. If he didn't live across the street from us, I don't think we'd hang out with him.

Cilla came back with three chipped mugs of vile burned liquid. Ev took his and grafted it with nondairy creamer and eight little packets of fake sugar, so much that the air around us turned sickly sweet.

Crock drank his coffee straight. I was afraid he might hurl again, but he kept it down. The guy could be a weasel, but his stomach was heroic. Most of the time.

As Evan doctored his coffee, I took the piece of paper out of my pocket, unfolded it, and laid it on the middle of the table. It was bright red with big black print. The letters had drops under them as though they were oozing blood. I let the others read it. I didn't need to. I had it memorized.

PfefferBrau Haus Presents
Grand Reopening, Saturday, April 26
We Want YOU to Wake the Dead
Do you have what it takes to rock the house?
Are you the Next Big Thing?

Apply to Jurgen and Arnold Pfeffer, Proprietors,
PfefferBrau Haus Brewpub
Prizes include: Gift Certificates to Jojo's Records,
Studio time,
Airplay on KGW-FM
Original music, please.

I watched their eyes scan the words, and waited for a reaction that wasn't long coming.

"*Wake the dead?*" Evan said. "Those twisted fucks."

By *twisted fucks* he meant the Pfeffer brothers. And he was right. They were totally twisted. They may not have been murderers (Idiot Willy said they were not "persons of interest"), but man, they had balls. *Wake the dead* was crass, even to me. And for a while, before we were the Gallivanters, I'd called our band Putrid Viscera. I was an expert on crass.

To know why it was so twisted, you'd have to know about Sherell Wexler, the only girl to be taken down from the Disappearing Wall.

She was the only one who reappeared.

Most of her, at least.

"You're not thinking of going to this, are you, Noah? That place is evil," Evan said.

Crock shrugged. "At least there's beer."

"Seriously? You'd actually drink that cannibal brew?"

That was the other thing you'd need to know about Sherell Wexler. The gruesome part. It was bad enough that she had her throat slit and her body dumped in a vat of porter, but the worst was that nobody found her right away.

First some customer in the PfefferBrau taproom found a long black hair in his stein. Then someone else found another. And then a third found something that looked like a fingernail, with *stuff* still attached to it. Finally the police were called in and Arnold Pfeffer, the younger Pfeffer brother and master brewer, drained the huge vat he'd nicknamed Hilda.

Some nights when I couldn't sleep (which was a lot), I couldn't help wondering: Did the beer level go straight down? Or was she clogging the drain at the bottom? Did they have to cut something off Sherell to get her out? A hand? A foot? A nose?

The police had the brewery cordoned off for weeks, drained every single piece of equipment in the entire place, but they didn't find anything or anyone else. Jurgen Pfeffer, the elder Pfeffer brother and big business brain, made a big stink about how they were cooperating but there was no evidence that he and his brother had done anything wrong, other than keeping lax security. It was obviously some sicko off the street who'd done it, and had we seen the size of the Pfeffers' operation? The skybridges? The grain elevators? The train tracks that led nowhere? Jurgen promised to make the points of ingress and egress more secure.

Whatever.

The upshot was that Sherell was accounted for and got a burial, and the rest of the girls remained Disappeared.

In my dark, black heart, I hoped Sherell didn't just drift gently and settle on the bottom. I wanted her body to thrash, a howl escaping from her beery, undead maw as she clung to some piece of machinery. Not because of the police, or for her parents, but for those two German freaks who had the nerve to advertise a poster like this.

Wake the dead, my ass.

Thinking about her, stewed into nothing, and Jurgen Pfeffer worried about something eating his *profits*, made me mad. I had a mission now. Never mind that it had been handed to me by some Bowie wannabe who I'd usually glare at and walk past.

"I want us to audition," I said.

Evan went bug-eyed. "Seriously?"

"Yeah, seriously," I said as I shredded my place mat into strips. I'd been away from my guitar too long. I needed something to thrash.

"Just the two of us?"

Ev on bass, me on lead guitar, just like old times. Even Crock had his uses. He was good at persuading. He used to be our manager. ("Sure. They're all twenty-one.")

But we were still only half a band.

Across the table, Ev and Crock stared at me, waiting for what they knew would come next.

"I was thinking of getting the Old Girls back."

There. I'd said it. We hadn't mentioned them since January, when Sonia had taken her drum kit out of my basement, loaded it into Jaime's car, and left.

I'd sat upstairs the whole time, wanting to plead with her to come back, but I didn't. Ev and Crock were there, waiting to see what I'd do, which was nothing. I wanted to go downstairs. I wanted to cry in front of her, slit my wrists, show her how desperate I was to get her back.

But I didn't. Instead, I listened as the two of them disassembled the kit, listening to the crash of the dropped hi-hat or the low bonk of the kettledrum. Evan whispered to me over and over that *I'd* been the asshole, and if I couldn't make it right, the least I could do was help them carry Sonia's crap out of my house. I told Ev that if he wanted to help, go right ahead. But I wasn't going to.

Look at the dog collar, I told him. Look at the shredded jeans. I didn't care about anything, least of all Sonia.

Now, in Denny's, Crock was the first to break the stare-off by laughing so hard coffee came out his nose. "*The Old Girls?* You're kidding, right?"

("I'm not cleaning up your coffee snot!" Cilla yelled across the restaurant, and tossed Crock a dishrag.)

Evan didn't quite join in the guffaw-fest. "Forget it, man. The Old Girls hate you."

"Not both of them," I said. "Just Sonia."

"Yes, but Jaime does whatever Sonia tells her," Ev said.

"She's still the weakling of the herd. I thought I'd pick her off first."

"They're not a herd." Ev shook his head. "Definitely not a herd."

He was right. There might've been two of them, but that didn't make them the same as each other or anyone else. Sonia was so spiky—her hair, her jean jacket, her attitude. That girl was unique—not to mention a master at pounding on stuff in a way that people couldn't look away from, the way her eyes bugged out and she sneered when she beat the shit out of any surface to make music.

I'd known her since seventh grade, and she was still cool—the last one I'd ever want to kill.

Crock read the flyer again. "April twenty-sixth. Less than two months away. They want original songs, Noah. Even if we get in, the Gallivanters are a cover band. Who's gonna compose?"

I fiddled with the crack in my mug, picking at it like a scab. "I've been kicking around a few ideas." Which was a lie. Until I'd seen the flyer earlier that night, I hadn't been kicking around anything at all. Except other kids in mosh pits.

But even if Ziggy hadn't said that thing about the coming darkness, I knew it was time to get my ass out of my basement and do something. Already I was imagining chords and driving rhythms, rearranging them in ways I hadn't heard anyone else do.

Why, when Ziggy said, *It has to be you*, I'd thought about my basement and the guitar gathering dust and the strings slowly warping out of tune, I don't know. Other than I'd been thinking about it a lot the past few months. All I needed was a nudge to froth over.

"All right," Evan finally said. "I get it. You want to get the band back together. But why do we have to play *there*?" He smacked the flyer. "Why can't we get a different gig?"

"It's actually not a bad idea," Crock said. "I mean, didn't you guys ever get tired of playing proms and weddings? We're all leaving by September anyway, right? Why not go out with a bang? Why not at least try to play the cannibal brewery? Don't tell me you guys have lost the dream of having your faces on flyers stapled to telephone poles. I mean, if you're serious, Noah, this could be it. We might be able to make actual money. You wouldn't have to sell any more plasma."

"We shouldn't do it, because we suck," Evan said evenly.

"Not necessarily." Crock shrugged. "I mean, yeah, a lot of what you did was crap. But you had your moments. A riff here, a growl there. And honestly, I keep telling you. If you really want to be popular, change your friggin' look. You won't pack clubs looking like crackheads. Even the Beatles had to clean up before they got famous."

"The Beatles are bland," Evan said.

"Shut up," I said.

"Sorry, man. Forgot how crappy you felt when Lennon died."

I stared at the flyer in the middle of the table. We all did. Then, slowly, Evan raised his eyes and said, "You can't help them, you know. They're already gone."

He wasn't talking about the Beatles.

He wasn't talking about Jaime and Sonia.

He was talking about the girls on the Disappearing Wall.

I had a rare, middle-of-the-night "I love you, man" moment for Ev, even though he understood just as much about my plan as I did, which was practically nothing.

I could see it in his overbright eyes and nicotine-stained teeth, and the hair he had to destroy so it could be art.

Here was why I needed to get the Gallivanters back together. *Here* was why it had to be a splashy gig—one that the entire city would remember for years. And that was why Ziggy had said, *It has to be you.*

It was because, in some way, Evan himself was slowly disappearing. I was the only one who could keep him from fading away.

I closed my eyes and thought about what to say to persuade them.

In the end, all I could do was open my mouth, and plead.

And even though it was the middle of the night and we all wanted nothing more than to be in bed, Ev took a deep breath and said, "All right."

I DIDN'T SLEEP SATURDAY NIGHT. Sunday around 8:00 P.M. I crashed on the sofa. At some point I stumbled to bed, still in the clothes I'd worn for two days. They smelled like smoke and bad coffee and meringue pies.

I dreamed about my dad again, the way he was before the accident. Jeans, a baseball cap, sturdy work boots, handlebar mustache. And the smirk. Oh god, the smirk. He was always a sanctimonious prick, even in real life. Why should he be any better in my nightmares?

In this one, he was standing at the top of the stairs, looking at me as I lay crumpled and helpless on the landing below. And even though his boots were on his feet, seven steps above me, I could feel those waffle-patterned soles stomping on my chest, crushing the air out of my lungs.

Daddy, no! Please! I'm sorry!

You think you're smart, do ya, punk ass? Lemme tell you something. You don't got brain one.

I woke to my clock radio. Or what would've been my radio if we got decent reception in my cul-de-sac. So it was more like I woke to static.

I opened one eye. It was dark out. That didn't mean anything. It was always dark when I got up for school. Whoever invented zero-hour classes should be shot.

I whacked the snooze button. Nothing happened, except the static got louder. *Kershshshsh . . .*

I whacked it again and again.

Finally I got a radio announcer voice.

Noah, it said. Then came the whirs and clicks, like it was tuning into a station.

"Go away," I groaned, jamming a pillow over my head.

Noah, it said. *Wake up. We've got work to do.*

My eyes snapped open. I knew that voice.

"Ziggy?" I said. I turned over. My clock read 3:15. My alarm was set, as usual, for 5:45. There was no more static. The house was silent. The night was silent. Which meant either I'd dreamed his voice or Ziggy had found a way to talk to me over the airwaves.

Had to be a dream.

Still, that didn't mean he wasn't right. I got up and sniffed my armpits. Ripe. Plus I was pretty sure one of my piercings was infected, 'cause I felt hot all over.

Whatever. I was awake now. Might as well get a head

start on the original songs we'd need if we were serious about joining the cannibal brewery lineup.

It was time for me to do what I'd been putting off since Sonia left.

I had to go back to the basement.

I tried hard not to let the basement freak me out. It was just a regular basement, right? Leaky fridge. Ugly plaid sofa. Mildew smell from when it flooded last year. Walls painted jaundice yellow, with a waterline marring the walls a foot off the floor.

The problem with the basement was that if you knew where to look (and I did), you could see a spot on the south wall where the yellow paint was peeling off. And under that, a splatter of brown that could've been anything. Mold. Bean dip. But it was neither of those things. It was a stain left over from Dad's "accident." The one everyone in town whispered about, but never to my face.

In daylight, I could spend the whole day in the basement and not even know the old blood was there. But at night? Even with all the lights on, I could feel it spread until it infected me. I even half expected Dad himself to leap out from behind the sofa. No matter how often I told myself I was being silly, that Dad was gone, some little piece of me was convinced that I hadn't been punished enough for what had happened, and he was going to make me pay, only this time he wouldn't stop. This time he'd go too far, and then *everything* would turn dark.

I tried not to think about it as I flipped on a light. See? No ghosts. Just my Fender on its stand by the sofa. I picked it up, plugged it in, put on my headphones so I wouldn't wake Mom and Cilla, and tuned up.

Now I could get down to the business of composing— but I couldn't shake my father's voice in my head.

Brain one. Punk ass.

I got up and flicked on more lights. I didn't want to think about my dad. I wanted to think about anything else.

I splayed the fingers on my right hand. The splints had been off for a month now, but my fingers had healed crooked. I hadn't played any serious licks or riffs since before the splints came off, and I didn't know if I still could.

If I really needed to write about something, I knew I should start with Sonia.

Right. About my fingers. And Sonia.

She and Jaime Deleuze were the two Old Girls. I don't think they even knew everyone called them the Old Girls. That name came from this freshman Elizabeth Kruk (never *ever* call her Liz or Lizzie).

Lizzie was a freshman I'd lip-locked with one night at a party in January. When I didn't call her the next day, or the day after that, and when she realized I wasn't going to call her at all, she cornered me by my locker and threw a very public hissy fit. "You don't want me," she'd said. "You only want the *old girls*."

I'd never thought of them that way, but Lizzie was right. Sonia and Jaime were the first girls in a school of two thousand who'd started trading their platform sandals for Doc Martens and changed their "schoolmarm of the prairie" dresses for ripped jeans and T-shirts.

Lizzie had some style, but she was a wannabe. There were exactly two cool girls in Gresham—and I'd pissed one of them off by making out with Lizzie at Todd Rathman's party.

Sonia and I were supposed to go together to Todd's party, but at the last minute her parents took her skiing at Mount Bachelor that weekend, so she wasn't around.

That was no excuse. Neither were the three or four PfefferBrau Pale Ales I'd slammed in a half hour. I knew what I was doing. Lizzie Kruk had a rack. And she was willing to let me touch it right there in Todd Rathman's living room. Over her shirt.

It was a good rack.

That shouldn't have mattered, but it did after a couple of PfefferBrau Porters. The point is, I'd been crushing on Sonia since the seventh grade, and after years of flirting and rides home and putting together the Gallivanters mostly to be with her—I'd even learned guitar 'cause I knew she was a drummer—she finally went out with me at the beginning of senior year. And once, when her parents were away, I even let her hook her cocker spaniel's leash to the studded dog collar around my neck and yank me where she wanted to go. *That* was how into her I was.

But wait! There's more! I locked lips with Lizzie on Todd's couch in front of about fifty people. At least twenty of them told Sonia the instant she got back.

She nailed me on a chilly morning when I was getting out of my car in the Gresham High parking lot. Her look was colder than the January rain. I made the mistake of saying, "It was just the one night. You can't really be mad at me for that." And she slammed the door on my fingers. My beloved Gremlin Ginny, used as a weapon.

For all you guys out there, take my word for it: Never tell a girl what they *can't* feel. Especially if that girl is a twitchy drummer. They like to pound stuff.

Here's my secret about the finger breakage: I *liked* it. I've always liked pain, especially if it came with something my teachers could see, like a black eye or a broken arm. When my dad was still living with us it meant he brought presents, like a new basketball or even my first electric guitar.

Not from Sonia. She kept punishing me. For weeks I drifted through the school halls with three fingers the size and color of bratwurst, strapped to metal splints, but Sonia pretended she didn't see me, like I was some kind of ghost.

Now, in my mildewed basement, I looked down at my guitar and realized I was strumming, and the sound that came out was so mournful you could hear the wail in another galaxy. I started humming the tune to what became "Gremlin Breakup." And yes, my fingers hurt, but the pain was delicious.

For the first time in months, I felt alive.

Bone breakage was one thing, dismemberment another. Since I wanted to keep the rest of my fingers attached to my hand, I figured that if I really wanted to get the Old Girls back in the band, I should talk to Jaime first. She wasn't twitchy. I'd never cheated on *her*. And the best time to catch her was after zero-hour class.

Only the real diehards were at school at 6:30 A.M., which meant stage band (me and Ev) and the Overtones Vocal Jazz (Jaime). Jaime didn't sing with the Overtones. She played keys, content to fade in the orchestra pit and let others have the spotlight.

As we spilled out of the band room that early Monday morning, Ev poked his head into the choir room next door. It was the same size as the band room, only cleaner, and the white walls were neatly painted with scores of treble and bass clefs. Even the choir kids, as they came trooping past, looked cleaner and brighter than the band geeks next door.

Inside, Jaime was being held back by Mr. Lehman, the director, who wanted to give her last-minute coaching. *You came in late, Jay. Less pedal. Crisper runs.*

And she stood there and took it, a weak smile on her face. That totally pissed me off. I mean, why did God invent punk if punks had to blindly suck up to authority?

Jaime was probably also the only girl in Gresham to be protected by the Gresham PD, because her mother was on the city council and had a public record of getting her way. Even though our 'burb was huge and sprawling, it was really a small town. There was a blanket order for Jaime not to hang out with punks like us. So of course she hung out with punks like us.

Once, after Jaime and I had been talking, smoking clove cigarettes on Main Street, Idiot Willy walked across the street and said, "Listen, man. I think you're all right. But *that woman* thinks you're a bad influence on her daughter. I'm supposed to invite you to go fuck yourself. Not in those words." He breathed out. He picked the earwax out of his ear. "Eh, screw it. Just be careful, Noah. I'll look the other way."

That woman was Jaime's mom, who was always harping on Jaime to give up the Gallivanters, to study harder and learn French and go to a good college on the East Coast and become a CEO, so she (Jaime) would never have to rely on a man to support her.

I personally thought that was unfair to Mr. Deleuze, who seemed like an okay guy. He was always on the cover of the *Gresham Outlook*, wearing a hard hat, pointing with blueprints to a new strip mall he was constructing.

True, we already had enough of them, but being a real estate developer didn't make Mr. Deleuze some useless trophy.

Ev and I stood at the threshold of the choir room. Jaime was backing away. She had permed, asymmetrical hair. The short side was pointed toward us. It made her neck look impossibly long, like a ballerina's. A ballerina in neon. She wore a dress of checks and stripes and acid tones. She may have been smiling politely, but she wore rage.

Good for her.

"Are you sure you don't want help talking to her?" Ev said. "She doesn't hate *me*."

"She doesn't hate anyone," I said. "I'll be fine."

Jaime was a famous pushover. I sometimes thought Sonia led *her* around on a leash. *Sure, Sonia. No prob, Sonia. Gee, I don't know if I should. I haven't asked Sonia yet . . .*

Finally Evan said, "Whatever. See you in personal finance." He took my guitar case and my car keys to drop our instruments in the Gremlin.

In the choir room, Jaime finally freed herself from Mr. Lehman.

She turned, saw me, and blushed brighter than her Day-Glo dress.

"Hey, Noah," she finally said. As she came closer, I read the button on her collar.

"'My karma ran over my dogma.' I like it," I said.

Jaime flashed a tired smile and muttered something about being late.

"I'll walk with you," I said. "I need to ask you something."

As we walked, I brought a finger up to the short side of her hair and set her plastic doll earring swinging back and forth from her earlobe. "Cool. Are those real dead babies?"

She flinched away from me. "Look, Noah, I think you're an okay guy and everything, but I don't want to be your go-between anymore," she said.

So sue me: It wasn't the first time I'd tried to use Jay to get to Sonia.

We were walking through the auditorium lobby, which had this run-down splendor. The foyer was carpeted in red velvet, the holes held together with silver duct tape. And there was that funky musty smell, the kind that came from layers of old paint and mildew and props that hadn't been used in fifty years.

"It's okay. I've given up trying to get her back. But . . ."

"Here it comes," she said.

". . . there's this thing at the PfefferBrau Haus . . ."

"What kind of thing?" I could almost see her cycle through a list, each item worse than the last: a party thing, a beer thing, a human-remains thing.

"The musical kind," I said.

I pulled the flyer from my pocket and handed it to her. She read it until after the second bell had rung and we were definitely late.

She ran her fingers over the paper, outlining the drops

of fake black blood. "I take it you want to pull Sonia and me in on this."

"Strictly business," I said. "I've given up on the personal stuff."

"Sure you have," she said.

I didn't say anything.

Jaime looked up. "I won't kid you. I think it'd be good for us. Sonia's parents won't let her practice in their garage, so she hangs out at my house all the time and we make cookies. *Cookies*, Noah. Always underdone, 'cause she's so twitchy she can't wait. She eats them raw. *Raw*."

I chose to ignore that last part, because it was dangerous to remember what Sonia was like raw.

Jay shook her head. "She's been trying to convince me to find another band. Any band but yours."

And despite the Day-Glo colors, I could've sworn that Jaime was slowly fading, blending in with the red velvet wallpaper.

"What about you? What do you want?" I said.

She considered, staring at nothing. She looked tired—as though someone had kept her awake all night, whispering commands in her ear.

"Out," she said.

I couldn't help sneering. It was what we all wanted. Only Jaime was getting it handed to her. Maybe not in the way she wanted—the scholarship, the poetry, the Republican-Nazi boyfriend—but she wouldn't be living in the suburbs for long.

She handed the flyer back to me. "I want this. Really I do. You've got vision, Noah. It's just that Sonia says . . ."

"What," I said. "Tell me what Sonia says."

Didn't matter. I'd heard it all before anyway.

"That you're not serious."

Jesus Christ. Fucking wannabe. Always doing whatever Sonia told her. It sucked that Jaime was a genius on the keys. Whether it was Beethoven or the Who, she put everything she had into those long fingers, the same ones that were handing me back my flyer.

"Forget it, Noah. It won't work."

"Yes it will," I said.

"How? What's changed? It's going to take more than one sick flyer to convince Sonia that this time you can keep us together. *All* of us."

We stood between two giant stairways winging up to the balcony. There was the sound of a match striking, then a small red glow. From the darkness of one of the stairways, a shape detached itself from the shadows and strutted forward.

I hadn't been expecting him, but I was glad he was here.

He led with the teeth, which weren't his best feature, all yellow and crooked. They made him look like a skull. The collar on his trench was flipped up, and he wore that confident Bowie sneer. His whole silhouette was wreathed in cigarette smoke, so his outline seemed to waver when you looked directly at him.

"Hello," Ziggy said in that suave musical lilt. "You must be Jaime."

Jaime looked as though she was about to jump out of her flat shoes. "There's no smoking in here," she said.

Ziggy kept puffing. He walked around her slowly, checking out the side view and the rear view and the front view.

When he'd made a full circuit, he brought a hand up to her earlobe. "Intriguing," he said. "Kewpie doll earrings. Pity 'bout your dress, though. Does nothing for you."

Jaime looked at her watch. "This is all very fun, but we're late."

And she started walking away.

Looking at her disappearing back, I got light-headed. I couldn't let her go, the way I did that day she and Sonia moved their stuff out of my basement.

It was time to care.

"Ziggy's our lead singer," I blurted. Which I didn't know. I just assumed that if he looked like the real Bowie, he must sound like him too.

And then a miracle happened.

Jaime came back to me. She wasn't as important to me as Sonia was, but for the moment, she was enough.

"What was that?"

"That's how you know we're serious. We've brought him in as a front."

Ziggy reached for her left hand, and she let him take it.

He turned it over in his palm, inspecting. I could almost feel the ridges of her bitten fingernails, the smoothness of her wrists, smell the citrus scent of her hand lotion. "Such clever fingers," he said to her, his voice low and seductive. "Your greatest gift and your greatest curse." He brought her palm up to his chest and massaged it, staring deep into her eyes. "You know what you need, don't you?"

"Enlighten me," she said.

"A voice," he whispered, loud enough for me to hear.

"Got a voice, thanks," she said. But it wasn't strong. He was weakening her.

She tried to pull away. He took a step forward, until she was smashed against the wall and he was leaning into her in a way that said, *I own you. You are* mine.

"You have many voices," he said with a half laugh. "I heard them just now. The Overtones, is it? They drown you out. Don't you want to be heard?"

"I'm not the genius," she said, but her voice wavered.

"Neither are the Overtones," Ziggy said.

At first I thought she was falling for it. She seemed completely lost in his face. Who could blame her? He was trotting out her deepest desire, stroking her hand, looking deep into her eyes. (Good work, man.)

But then she broke away. "Oh-ho. Nice try. But there's a reason the Gallivanters broke up. What makes you think this time will be different?"

He leaned in close and whispered something in her

ear. I really didn't like him treating her like, you know, a girl. If he was going to be in the band, the rule was hands off the Old Girls. I'd learned my lesson. We couldn't afford any more breakages.

He pulled away and shot me a look that said, *It's in the bag.*

Jaime turned to me, and I looked past her Day-Glo dress and poodle hair and saw how she used to be: the second-to-last girl I would kill in Mafia, the first of the Old Girls Evan would save.

"How sick?" she said.

Ziggy had told her about Evan. I wanted to say, "No worse than usual," but held back, because it wasn't true. Ev's headaches were getting worse. A lot worse.

I must've been really tired from the night before, because my vision blurred, and then everything went double. There were two Jaimes, two entrances to the auditorium—but only one Ziggy, who faded in and out, like noise from a radio station not properly tuned.

I felt dizzy, as though I were about to fall over.

"Noah?" she said. "How sick?"

At first I thought she was talking about me, weaving on my feet, seeing everything double. In the end, all I could do was shut my eyes and listen for the deeper truth.

"He needs this," I said. "We all do."

THE OLD GIRLS WEREN'T COMING.

I'd told Jaime to meet at my house at 2:00 on Sunday. It was now 2:05.

I tried to tell myself it didn't matter. It was a sunny afternoon. Ev and Crock and I were hanging out in my driveway. They were shooting hoops and I was cleaning my car. Same as it ever was.

I asked the two of them to please keep the basketball from bouncing on Ginny's hood, and they said why don't you move her to the street, and I said because it's my driveway, and why don't you shoot hoops at someone else's house for once?

Yeah. It was a nice try, but we all knew they couldn't leave. Home for Crock meant his stepdad, Idiot Willy, who didn't like him and who kept live ammo around the house. Home for Ev meant his house at the top of Walter's Hill, where his mom tried to dress him to coordinate with her chintz sofa. They both preferred my house, even though it was haunted.

The basketball bounced once onto the pavement, then ricocheted onto Ginny's bumper. "Sorry," Ev said, not sorry at all. "So, are we going to see Ziggy today or not?"

I stopped buffing Ginny's hood. "How do you know about him?" I hadn't said anything to them. It didn't seem worth it until the Old Girls signed on.

"Jaime told him," Crock said. *Swish!* He fired a jumper from three-point land (my lawn). The ball went straight through the net.

"Yeah? What else did she tell you?"

Ev lined up another outside shot, and I could tell it was going to miss. It was going to dent my car. So, like a dumb-ass, instead of going for the rebound directly, I threw myself on Ginny's hood, shielding her from the ball.

Then, of course, as I was spread out like that, looking like a doofus, I heard the purr of an engine and lifted my head in time to see the girls pull up in Jaime's parents' Volkswagen Rabbit.

I stood up real quick.

I watched Sonia unfold herself, colt-like, from the passenger side, and everything from my head to my nuts slid and jolted so hard it felt like my guts were doing a slam dance.

She was one long, thin girl. Her brown eyes were the size of 45s. She had teased-up black hair and a skinny, grabbable rattail of a braid that had grown a couple of inches since we'd been together. Now it was glossy and sleek like a whip, and it hung over her left shoulder and reached down to the crevice between her boobs. I wanted to kiss the length of it like I used to. I wanted to feel the crack of it across my face.

She came closer and I inhaled her scent, all musky, like cinnamon and damp earth.

I didn't realize I was shaking until Ev put a hand on my arm in a *be cool* gesture.

I shoved my hands in my pockets and walked toward the girl of my life. "Hey," I said. "I'm glad you—"

She held up her palm like a traffic cop. "Why didn't you tell Jaime about the money?" she said.

"What money?"

"Oh yeah," Crock said. "I made some calls. There's a purse. Not just airplay and studio time."

"How big?" I said.

"Fifteen hundred dollars," Crock said.

Money. Why hadn't I thought of that? Of course that would reel her in. Sonia's dad was a self-made man with a chain of appliance stores. He wasn't big on spreading his cash around, though. So while the Krajiceks had a condo at Mount Bachelor and another one in Cabo San Lucas, Sonia would have to work her way through college. Her dad acted like he was doing her a big favor, but you could tell he cared less about her than about sipping cabernet in a hot tub somewhere.

Meanwhile, Jay was getting out of the car from the other side, wearing an outfit so bright and polka-dotted she looked like Minnie Mouse.

"It's not a lot if you split it five ways . . ." Crock went on.

"Six," I said. "We've got Ziggy now."

Sonia's record-sized eyes popped out a little more, and she shot Jaime a look. "You want us to split our prize money with him? Isn't that taking it a little far?" she said.

I thought about saying, *It was his idea. He deserves a cut.* But I looked at my ex, who was here in front of me but already backing away, and I screwed Ziggy completely.

"You're right," I said. "We can probably talk him into working pro bono."

Another snort from Crock.

After what seemed like a beat too long, Jaime asked Sonia quietly, "Should we go in?"

"I got Milk Duds. And Tab," I said. I knew it was her favorite snack combo. She loved picking Duds out of her teeth.

"All right," she said at last. "As long as you know I'm in it for the money. This is just business. Understand?" She jabbed me in the chest.

My crooked fingers ached with longing. I wanted her to hurt me over and over again.

"Sure. No prob."

• • •

I led them all down to the basement. Ev's eyes flicked to the spot on the wall where the stain was showing through. He'd been here the day of Dad's accident too.

Everyone else rushed ahead to their stations.

Ev's bass and my guitar were on stands in the corner by the amp, next to the upright piano with faux wood paneling. I figured Sonia wouldn't be "in" enough to bring her kit, so I found upturned paint buckets and a Folgers Crystals coffee can. As I may have mentioned: Sonia can beat on anything.

Crock found the food.

He pulled a six-pack of Tab from the drippy basement fridge and set it on the Formica coffee table, along with a tray of tea sandwiches (peanut butter and grape jelly) and a carefully arranged pyramid of Milk Duds.

"Did you really cut the crusts off these?" Crock said, double-fisting the sandwiches.

I nodded. "Dud?" I offered Sonia.

"Those things look like rabbit poop," Crock said, his mouth sticky and his speech slurring from the peanut butter.

"They're not for you, ass-wipe," I said. Crock kept eating.

There was a tinny, out-of-tune clang. Jay was testing the piano. She played a couple of runs that sounded classical. Probably Beethoven. It was Jaime's version of warming up.

She played the runs again, but she began to change the beat, put a little hesitation in it. 1–2, 1–2–3. Waiting until the last moment to play the next note. That little bit of syncopation gave it a Latin feel.

Sonia, meanwhile, found the coffee can and started shaking it like a maraca.

I opened a Tab and sipped, closing my eyes. *Do you hear it?* I heard Ziggy's voice in my head. *Do you hear how it could be?*

Yes, I thought. *Yes and yes and yes.* My buddies were weaving a kind of Latin magic around me. Ev and me could pick it up at any time and words would follow. Two verses. A bridge. A chorus.

Then it was over with a shriek.

"Stop it, stop it, *stop it!* Do you have any idea what time it is?"

Cilla came down the stairs wearing nothing but an oversized football jersey, her bleached hair sticking up in a rat's nest, the skin under her eyes thin and purple. She looked like someone's tragic heroin-addicted girlfriend.

Sonia and Jay stopped playing.

"Do you know how late I worked this morning?"

It was a rhetorical question. Any time of day or night was too late for her.

"You," my sister went on, glaring at Sonia. "What the hell are you doing here? You said Noah was an asshole and you were better off without him, remember?"

"It's just business," Sonia said in such a soft voice it sounded as though her mouth was jammed with peanut butter. Which it wasn't.

"Whatever," Cilla said. "Look, if you want to start up with my brother again, be my guest. Break more fingers. Break anything you want. I don't care. But you can't practice here. I work nights. You guys almost drove me to the loony bin last time."

I felt rage wash over me. My hands balled into fists at my sides.

"Why don't you move out, then?" I said.

She glared at me. "What?"

I felt the leather of my square-toed boots thicken. I wanted to stomp her into chunky salsa. "I said: Why don't you move out?"

Jay closed the lid on the highball piano, with the watermarks from years of our parents' guests setting down their scotch and sodas, and looked at a watch she wasn't wearing. "Sonia and I have to study," she said. "Personal finance." Then she mumbled something that sounded like "worth half a grade."

Sonia shuffled her feet, then swept some Milk Duds directly into her purse. "See you, Noah," she said.

Crock and Ev followed them, muttering blah blah ride home blah blah blah, even though Crock only had to go across the street.

I heard the front door open and close.

Fuckin' A. I'd almost done it. I'd actually gotten us back

together, for five whole minutes. Then my stupid-bitch sister ruined it.

She started shrieking even before the front door closed. "What gives you the right to boss me around?"

"Easy. You're twenty-one years old. You've got a job. You don't pay rent and you never do the dishes."

"I do the dishes. I do the dishes plenty."

"—I mow the lawn. I vacuum—"

"—I'm up late working hard. Not something *you'd* understand."

And then I did it. The one thing I vowed I'd never do.

I pushed her.

This was no mosh pit. There was no one behind her to help her up. She fell backward onto the stairs, and even though she didn't crack her head, she might as well have. That look of wild-eyed fear that came over her—I'd seen it many times before, but never pointed at me.

It only lasted a second, then she was back to being the Cilla I knew, the boss of me and untold legions of shiftless truckers, and I was back to being Noah, the kid who looked tough but who never ever fought back.

"Please. Don't say it," I begged.

She got to her feet, and even though she was my height, she towered over me. "You're no better than *Dad*."

That was all I could take. I ran past her up the stairs, outside, and into Ginny, feeling like I was never going to breathe again.

• • •

I drove aimlessly, thinking, *What have I done?*

If there was one thing I'd learned living with an abusive asshole, it was how to avoid one. Most of the time you can find a corner to hide in until the booze wears off, or payday comes, or they bag a black-tailed deer, or their football team wins the Rose Bowl, or whatever they need in order to feel good about themselves again and don't have to take their shitty life out on *you.*

But that was no help today. What happens when *you're* the abusive asshole?

Where do you hide from yourself?

5

I WOUND UP AT THE CINEMA 21, an art house theater in northwest Portland. I liked to go to that neighborhood because it was what Mom called "in transition." Meaning Heidi's Olde Worlde Pastries had vacated the chalet-type building, and a General Gao's Szechuan Garden had moved in. There were ancient apartment buildings with rats in the dumbwaiters next door to brightly lit Austrian bakeries.

The Cinema 21 might have been due for an overhaul, but so far no one had tried. And honestly? I liked it the way it was. Reliable. Same neon starburst marquee, same bottomless popcorn for seventy-five cents a bag.

That night they were showing *Merry Christmas, Mr. Lawrence*. It was supposed to be a good flick but I hadn't seen it yet, because it was a Bowie movie.

I was sick of Bowie by then. He was on every poster in

every girl's locker, an impossible standard to live up to. But there was something comforting about him too. He changed everything about himself, his hair and makeup and name and even his voice, but he kept something in each. Self-assurance. Calm.

Even in the movie, when Bowie is supposed to be a suicidally brave POW in a World War II prison camp—with bad hair (*shyeah*, right)—and he's locked in a cage, muttering the words "I wish I could sing," because his character supposedly can't, there's this larger-than-life presence. He would never hit his sister. He would never cheat on his girlfriend . . . Well, yeah, he might, but at least he'd do it with style.

Dad used to hate Bowie. We watched him on TV once when I was little, and Bowie was in his Aladdin Sane phase then, with spiky red hair and a spandex jumpsuit. I don't remember what he sang. Some song about space. Or was it loneliness? The way he sang, it was the same thing.

Dad pulled on his beer that looked like golden water and said, "Do me a favor and change it to the Blazers game, will ya, son? I can't stand watching that faggot."

Since I was just a kid, I didn't know what "faggot" meant, other than *not Dad*. Which seemed like a good thing.

Even now, when I was eighteen, *not Dad* was something I had to work hard at every day. When my hair started coming in thick and dark like his, I dyed it green.

When people started bugging me, I went to the mosh pit to thrash it out before I thrashed them.

Today was my first big fail.

I had hit someone I loved. She was bossy and ambitionless, but I still loved her.

For two hours during the movie, I thought it might be possible that I could still be a hero, like Bowie's character. But then the closing credits rolled, and ended, and a different kind of picture looped in my mind—one of me pushing my sister, over and over again.

Why did she have to keep picking at me? *Do this, nimrod. Do that, nimrod.* Sometimes I hated her.

But I never hit her.

What was Cilla doing now? Blabbing to Mom? Blabbing to any Denny's trucker about how I was turning out just like Dad? The instant she did, the half of the state that hadn't already written me off would write me off. I would go from being an asshole to being "just like my father."

That was something I wanted to avoid at all costs.

Outside the theater, a light rain had started to fall, making my mohawk flop over. Green dye trickled down my forehead and into my eyes, making everything look like an alien landscape from some cheesy sci-fi movie. I was walking past the narrow employees' parking lot behind the theater. I remember thinking, *I wish I could get out of my skin for more than two hours*, when I first felt the chill.

It wasn't a regular cold chill, or even a flu chill. It was

worse than that. I'd felt it once before, when I'd been so terrified it felt like my blood had frozen.

There was a scuttling noise, then a high-pitched squeak, like a dozen rats on the move.

Noah.

Someone was calling me, and it didn't sound like Ziggy.

I stopped and looked. There was a line of beat-up cars, Pintos and Pacers, and behind that was a dumpster overflowing with stale popcorn and Red Vines and Junior Mints.

I couldn't see beyond the dumpster. It was too dark. But—and this was the weird thing—the darkness had an edge. There was normal stuff in front of it, cars and garbage cans, then just nothing. Whatever was calling me was inside that dark fog bank.

Noah, it said again.

I sniffed the air. Hops. It smelled really strongly of cooking hops.

Slowly, the dark cloud rolled closer. Whatever it touched looked as though it disappeared, as if the cloud swallowed it whole.

Clouds didn't freak me out. We had clouds that belched rain, hail, pollution, radioactive isotopes (Trojan Nuclear Plant)—even volcanic ash (Mount St. Helens).

But there was something different about this one—and it wasn't just the smell. First, there was the frost, which seemed to inject itself right into my heart and spread through my veins. If I wasn't still breathing, I would've thought I'd been turned to ice. But breathe I did, and dark green clouds came out of my nose like frozen bile.

This cloud was poison. And it was sucking me in.

Noah!

The voice was more urgent now.

Let me whisper in your ear. Let me tell you what I've already done and what I'm about to do to everyone you love.

The cloud came closer with a skittering noise, advancing, retreating, changing shape, as though something inside it—several things—were fighting to get out.

Help us, Noah!

Girls' faces, half formed, came to the front.

And then that whispering, disembodied voice again: *Shall I tell you about them? How they died alone and afraid? Their terror fed me. It made me strong.*

Slowly, I started to back away. I was getting sick, that was it. I hadn't been sleeping enough. No wonder I was imagining things.

Watch, Noah. Witness.

Then came the one I'd been fearing. The girl from the poster without a name or a reward or Last Seen Wearing. I knew what she was going to say.

Please!

Oh god. I wasn't sick. I wasn't sleep-deprived. That thing—that toxic darkness—had consumed the Disappearing Girls.

I should've run. But I couldn't move. I could only stand and watch what I half knew was coming next.

When *Please* Girl's face disappeared, another didn't appear right away. The inky darkness started to twirl, then locked itself into dreads. Another face flashed across the front of the cloud, screwed up in agony. I heard the scream from my head clear down to my toes.

That thing had Evan.

I didn't even think. I charged forward. "Hey!" I said. "Let him go!"

I hadn't gone two steps before—*bam!*—I tripped on a speed bump and went down hard, banging my forehead on asphalt.

Red blood and green dye dripped into my eyes like an insane Christmas garland. I needed to see what was going on, but my head was so heavy it was like an anchor.

I had to get to my feet and charge that cloud. I had to save my friend.

Help me, Noah!

And then, from somewhere above me, came a light. It was golden and warm. "Sing, lad!" it commanded.

Not golden light, I realized. Yellow. Egg-yolk yellow.

"Huh?"

"Sing! Sing *now!*" And that was when I realized my pounding head had a backbeat. Without looking up, I opened my mouth and sang about fear, and failure, and all the things I'd been worrying about for most of my life.

If I had to give the song a title, I would've called it "You Don't Got Brain One."

I was too confused even to stand up, but all the ways I'd failed people? *That* I remembered.

I sensed the thing stopping. I closed my mouth and wiped the red rain from my eyes. I managed to get to my knees and look up. I hoped I wasn't too late.

The dark cloud had retreated. It hovered behind the dumpster, waiting for something—I didn't know what.

It wasn't calling to me anymore, wasn't screaming, and there were no faces inside. But it was still dangerous. And it still had Evan.

Ziggy gripped me by the forearm and helped me to my feet. "You okay, lad?"

I charged forward. "That thing has my friend!"

He locked my arm with his tiger grip. I couldn't shake him off. "It's not that simple. You can't take it on directly or it'll swallow you too."

"I can't just leave him there!"

"Easy, old boy. The Marr hasn't swallowed him completely. Not yet. He's safe in bed. If you called him at home right now, you'd get him. He'd wonder why you woke him up."

"I don't understand. I just saw his face!"

"The Marr can work slowly, son. It can take its victims a piece at a time."

I put my hands on my knees and sucked air. "So he's fine?"

Ziggy didn't say anything. He wouldn't meet my eyes.

Even though I was so freaked out I was sweating poison, I started to take in more details of the monster cloud.

Clack! I thought I saw a claw reaching out, testing.

"How do we get rid of it?"

He shook his head. "You mean completely? Don't be stupid." He pronounced it *shtyou*-pid. "You can never get rid of the Marr. It's a part of life."

I sniffed the air. The hops smell intensified. Slowly, that thing, that Marr, began to creep forward again.

"All the same, best not to stick around," Ziggy said, and pulled me by the elbow down the street. "Come on, son. Time to regroup and form a battle plan."

"Sure. Just a sec." I turned around and flipped that thing off.

Yeah. I know. Real mature, not to mention dangerous. But damn did it feel good.

I'D NEVER BEEN INSIDE COFFEE INVASION BEFORE, but I'm pretty sure that, like a lot of places I found that muggy spring, it had been there all along, and it only *seemed* to pop up when we needed it.

It was two blocks away from Cinema 21 and was the first place Ziggy and I ran to, trying to escape that thing by the dumpster. What had he called it? The Mars? There was no life on Mars. Or at least none that clacked and sucked the hope right out of you. I'm sure there were people who believed that shit, but those were the same guys who thought they saw Elvis in the Piggly Wiggly five years after he died.

When Ziggy and I ran into Coffee Invasion that night, I felt like I'd made it to home base and that whatever that thing was, no way it could tag us now. The café was too clean and bright, and what the hell was that smell? Could it be . . . *coffee*?

I wouldn't know, since my only experience of the stuff was the crystals my mom shoveled straight into her mouth and the sludge they served at Denny's.

Coffee Invasion was like a whole different world. The customers looked like they actually wanted to be there. There were couples wearing velvet and spooning cheesecake into each other's mouths. The pastry case facing the front door displayed desserts that actually looked like fruit and chocolate instead of . . . I don't know, gelatin and marshmallows and cigarette butts.

While I was looking around, I hadn't noticed the girl. But there was one, not much older than me, standing behind the front counter. She had brown curly hair and a scrubbed face that looked like it belonged on a student government poster. She was staring at me. "You're bleeding," she said.

"What? Oh." I touched the growing boulder on my forehead. It was tender and sticky with blood. I'd forgotten about my collision with the speed bump. I must've looked a nightmare. I was bringing the whole tone of the place down. "Sorry about that. We can leave."

"Don't be silly. You're the first customer we've had younger than forty for . . . ever," she said, smiling brighter than the neon sign out front. "Right this way."

She showed us to a round café table by the window,

with a clear view of the street. Perfect. Above our heads was a neon sign of a cup of coffee with arms and legs and jagged teeth chasing B-movie victims. Ha-ha. Very funny. It was on a timer, because it buzzed on and off with a loud *zzzt*.

The girl with the curly hair handed me a menu, completely ignoring Ziggy, and said, "I'm guessing coffee, right?"

Ziggy nodded.

"Please. Two," I said.

She looked at me intently. "Been that kind of night, has it? No prob." She disappeared through a set of chrome doors that squeaked behind her as they swung shut.

As soon as she was gone, I chanced a look outside. It was dark, but normal dark. Not sucking-wound-in-the-fabric-of-the-universe dark.

I began to breathe.

I leaned forward and asked Ziggy, "Are we safe?"

"For now," he said. He unbuttoned his silk jacket and crossed his legs. He lit a cigarette, took a drag, and time slowed. I wished I smoked. It had a profound effect on people who knew how to do it. Which I didn't. I always choked and hacked up loogies. Plus Dad had smoked a lot. One more reason for me never to learn.

"What did you call that thing, anyway? A Mars?"

"'Marr,' son. No *s* on the end. Two *r*s."

"What the hell is it? It felt like pure evil." I could still hear the screams of *Please* Girl and see the shadowy look on her face as it flashed in front of the cloud.

Ziggy shook his head. "It's beyond evil. Is a tiger evil? No, son. It's a predator. Only, the Marr's not a very efficient one. It tends to decimate what it hunts. It consumes without stopping."

I asked the obvious question. "Then why did you hold me back? That thing has Evan."

"Because, lad. You can't take on the thing head-on. It would've gotten you too, and we never would've been able to get you out. It's different with your mate. It only got pieces of him. There may still be time to save him."

"Oh yeah? Enlighten me. How do we do that?"

Ziggy looked on the verge of answering, but the hostess came back with two teeny-weeny cups of coffee, a stack of napkins, and a slice of something chocolate. It was swimming in a pool of red sauce on a clear glass plate.

Oh god. That had better not be what it looked like.

"Here you go. Two espressos for your tough night. Napkins for your head. And . . ." She looked over her shoulder at the kitchen beyond the pastry case. When it seemed like no one was looking, she shoved the plate at me.

"I didn't ask for this," I said, trying not to sound as freaked as I was.

"I know."

"What is it?"

"Chocolate ganache." She did a back-check again.

"Chocolate what?"

"Ganache. Go on. Take a bite."

"Is this expensive? Cause I don't . . ."

A gray-haired woman came into view behind the counter. The hostess ducked low.

"Quick. Try it now."

"What? Why?"

"Please. I don't have much time. Take a bite."

I made a quick judgment call then. No girl with a face as scrubbed as that could be pushing me to eat chocolate in a pool of human blood. I picked up the fork and shoved some in my mouth.

And oh, the way that chocolate whatsit melted. It made me feel like there were no dumpsters in the world, and I could walk down the street without worrying about anything—least of all Evan—ever again.

"Jesus," I said.

"What? What's wrong?"

"It's addictive. Are those raspberries?" I swirled designs in the red pool.

And that girl smiled brighter than Ziggy's hair. "Oh yeah. I strained them myself. Through a cheesecloth and everything. Do you really like it? 'Cause I was worried that it might be a little too bitter—"

"Excuse me, sir, but how do you intend to pay for that?"

The gray-haired woman was now standing over us. She had on an apron over a flowered dress that made her arms look pillowy, like pastry dough.

She looked me over, my green hair and forehead dripping blood, and smiled a tight smile.

I looked at Ziggy. Wasn't it obvious that the suave man chain-smoking in the thousand-dollar suit would pay?

"Ah, crap," the girl said, standing up. "It's not a big deal, Mom. It's just the chocolate ganache cake I made. You were going to throw it out anyway 'cause it turned out lopsided."

"It didn't taste lopsided," I said.

Another tight smile from her mother. "You're too kind. Can I speak to you for a second, Claire?" She pulled her daughter over to the pastry case and whispered to her loudly enough that I heard the words "bringing down the tone" and "feeding every skate punk that comes through" and "go broke."

I didn't understand. I was used to this treatment in Gresham, where everyone knew my history and was just waiting for me to turn out like my dad. But no one knew me here. Besides, I was eating with Ziggy, who, if anything, brought up the tone of the place.

They were still arguing when I decided I would stay put until they kicked me out. It had already been a long night, and the chocolate cake was so good I was beginning to feel safe again. "You don't want a bite of this, do you, Ziggy?"

"That's quite all right, old boy. You need it more than I do. Your first glimpse of the Marr. I'm surprised your hair hasn't turned white." He scooted his chair closer. "Tell me, lad. What did you see in it?"

"You know what I saw," I said, my mouth gummed up with chocolate. "I saw my friend Evan."

"And?" Ziggy prompted.

"Isn't that enough?"

"One face? It might be. Some see just one. But you saw more, didn't you? You're different."

"Why? What makes me different?"

He tapped out his cigarette in the saucer in front of him. He knew. I don't know how he found out about Dad's accident, but he knew.

Had he been stalking me? I was already starting to think that running into him that night in front of the PfeferBrau Haus, when I was out of options and needed someone most, was no accident.

Whose side was he really on?

He could be evil. But he was in here with me, and the Marr was out there. I didn't know what to think. Why could I see the Marr when others couldn't? Not for the first time, I wondered, was I sick? Did I need to be locked up?

I set down my fork, suddenly full. "I'm damaged, aren't I?"

For a second, I'd forgotten the world outside. But now it came crashing down around me. Why couldn't I just live here, in Coffee Invasion, not in a split-level on a dead-end street in the suburbs? Why was I the only one to see patterns on cork walls in Denny's, shadows behind the dumpsters of run-down theaters?

"Come now, lad. We both know you've had more than your share of blows in your life. Can you honestly tell me you think the same way as the rest of these fine citizens?"

He nodded toward the people in the café. They wore silk and discreet jewelry. They ate cheesecake and pear tarts. And by the pastry case, one girl named Claire was getting nailed for using me as a guinea pig for her cooking experiments, a crime that was probably not going to get her pushed down a flight of stairs.

"No. They don't see the danger."

"Exactly." Ziggy nodded. "Now, tell me, Noah. What did you see?"

I braced myself with coffee from the teeny-weeny cup. I let the warmth and taste invade my body from my head to the tips of my fingers. "I saw girls. A lot of them. The ones who've disappeared around the city," I said.

It was crazy. But I was beyond caring what I sounded like.

Ziggy leaned back in his chair. "Oh my," he said.
"What?"

"You're more in tune with the Marr than I thought."

"I take it that's not a good thing."

Ziggy considered, and tugged on his expensive cigarette.

"I don't understand. You were standing right next to me. Why didn't you see the Disappearing Girls too?"

"The Marr presents itself in different ways to different people. I don't share your experience."

"Why? What do you see?"

I looked into his eye that was all pupil. Nothing good could come of someone with an eye like that. That thing could be a tunnel to hell.

"Too much, son. I see masses of people in pain. But the pain isn't the worst part."

"What is?"

He picked a fleck of something off his upper lip and rolled it in distaste. "That day in the basement, Noah, the split second before the gun went off, do you remember what you felt?"

My hands clenched around a napkin. I wasn't amazed that he knew about the accident. It was just that I'd tried so long to block it out of my memory.

It never worked.

The accident itself took less than a second. But in all the seconds leading up to it, even though the gun was pointed away from me, it was still in Dad's hands. There was nothing to keep him from turning it around. And even if he didn't, even after all the things he'd done to me and my family, I still didn't want to lose him.

You think you're smart, don't ya, punk ass? You'll never be free.

I pushed away my plate, even though there was half a slice left. "Fear," I said.

I remembered that part vividly. The fear had frozen my blood. I'd felt like I couldn't move my arms or legs. And I was so cold. I'd never felt as cold since. Until tonight.

Ziggy picked up my fork and sampled the chocolate ganache. He left me the darkest part on the bottom, rich and bitter at the same time. "All right," I said. "The Marr isn't evil. It feeds on fear. So what can we do to make people less afraid?"

Ziggy's eyes focused on something on the street outside. "Oh lord."

"What? What is it?"

There was no darkness creeping down the street. Just four people. Two men and two women in expensive overcoats, their collars turned up against the rain.

Whatever color had been in Ziggy's face instantly drained. "I should've known. This is one of the few cafés open late Sunday nights. He's not the type to turn in early on any day of the week."

"He who?"

But I knew who, even before I could make out the details of the guy's craggy face, with eyebrows so thick and furry he looked like a wolf.

"Jurgen Pfeffer," I said. "You think he's got something to do with the Marr, don't you?"

"Lad," Ziggy said, leaning toward me and whispering. "He's *brewing* it. And it's spreading."

I sniffed the air. A new scent was mingling with the coffee and chocolate and raspberries. I felt fingers of cold scuttle up and down the fine hairs of my neck.

My eyes shot from the men in the entrance to where our teenage hostess was still listening to her mother tell her in a quiet voice exactly how she'd screwed up.

"You know what you have to do," Ziggy said.

I was on my feet before he stopped talking. I went up to the pastry case. "Excuse me, ma'am?" The mother turned to me. "I need to speak with you for a second."

She shot her daughter a look that said *You're gonna get it later*, then walked around to face me. "What do you want?"

I took her doughy arm. "Get your girl out of sight right now. Quick. Before they see her."

I nodded at the entrance, at the ones who just came in. First came Jurgen Pfeffer, with his sharp blue eyes and craggy face, flanked by two girls with eye shadow clear out to their temples.

And following behind them, not flanked by any girls at all, was Jurgen's other half, Arnold, the brother the papers ironically dubbed "Little Pfeffer," even though Arnold looked like a Pfeffer-and-a-half standing behind his brother, since he was a foot taller and twice as broad. He had icy blond hair cut into a flattop, and his chest was so sculpted it looked like he had two muscled boobs.

I've gotta hand it to her: The woman with the doughy arms was cool. She stood in front of her daughter and slowly backed the two of them toward the chrome kitchen doors. They were gone for a while.

Meanwhile, I found myself standing alone behind the front counter.

Jurgen Pfeffer snapped his fingers in my face. "Boy. Do you work here?" He pronounced it "verk."

My eyes went to cubbies under the desk. I found the menus I was looking for. "Table for four? Right this way, sir."

I didn't know if there were any tables for four. But I looked around and found one far, far away from the kitchen.

I sat them down and handed each of them a menu. I didn't know anything about being a hostess, so I tried to remember what the girl had said. And it wasn't so much what she'd said as the ease with which she'd said it.

"I'm assuming coffee all around?" The girls nodded their empty heads, but Jurgen sized me up.

"You don't really verk here, do you?"

At our table by the front window, Ziggy sat calmly smoking. Why wasn't *he* doing this? Why was I stuck handling this German asshole?

"How do you know?" I said.

He pointed at my forehead.

"You're bleeding. The health department frowns on human blood in food. And I would know." And the sicko laughed. And his two dates laughed with him. But seated in the corner, with his back to the wall, Little

Pfeffer didn't laugh. He didn't smile. He wore a haunted expression that I was oh so familiar with from looking in mirrors when my father was alive. It was an expression that said, *I don't think this is right, but what do I know? I'm worthless.*

What, I wondered, did Jurgen have on him that Little Pfeffer had to follow his brother around like a puppy? The papers said Arnold cried for days over Sherell Wexler, some random kid he didn't even know.

If he could just stand up to his twisted brother, I'd feel a whole lot better about our Wake the Dead gig.

And suddenly, I knew what to say. "You're right," I told Jurgen. "I don't work here. I was just having coffee when I saw you come in. I'm a musician. I need a break. I thought I'd take a shot."

Jurgen's face took a serious turn. He studied me as though I was a difficult exercise in translation.

"I see," he said. "And you think we can give it to you?"

"I don't expect you to just hand it to me," I said. "I intend to work for it."

It was only half a lie. I didn't tell him that I wanted it for my sick friend. I didn't tell him that if only he would let me into the brewery, I would find the Marr, somehow reach into it, pull out the pieces of Evan, and put him back together.

"I see. You and half the city," he said. "People are very forgiving when fame is at stake." He reached into the inside pocket of his jacket and pulled out a silver case, from which he removed a business card. "When you have your demo, go ahead and send it to me personally with a note. Remind me that you're the boy from Coffee Invasion. Now, will you please send over our real waitress? Or are you hiding her in the back?"

I almost ruined it then. I almost bounced him, with a *Get out of here and don't come back, you sick fuck*, but I didn't have to. Because one of the dates, a blonde, answered for me. She laughed a fake laugh. "Oh, Jurgy. Who would want to hide from you?" There was fawning. There was nose wrinkling. There was hair twirling. Even Lizzie Kruk herself could take a lesson in skankiness from this jumpsuited, shoulder-padded fluff brain.

The girls laughed. Pfeffer laughed.

Little Pfeffer did not. He looked ashamed. He didn't even open his mouth, but I knew that, even though he was ripped, that didn't make him a big dumb jock.

I took Jurgen's business card as though it were gold. "Yes, sir. Right away, sir."

Ziggy was still sitting at our table at the front window, but I couldn't get to him right away. That doughy woman, the mother of the girl Claire, grabbed me by the wrist and took a damp washcloth to my head.

"What did they say?" she whispered.

"They want a real server," I said. "I'm sorry. I tried."

And that woman wrapped me in her doughy embrace. I couldn't help thinking of the phrase *pig in a blanket*.

Which made me a pig, but I didn't care. I loved the blanketing part.

"You're a good boy. Would you please stay until they're gone? I'd feel so much better. Order whatever you want. It's on the house."

"No need," I said. Of course I'd stay. I would've done it anyway, because Jurgen Pfeffer reminded me so much of my father. No one should have to put up with that.

But then something happened that made the decision easier.

After Pfeffer's comment about hiding a waitress in the back, I knew I shouldn't look at the chrome doors that led to the kitchen, but I did anyway. There were two small rectangular windows toward the top. One moment nothing was there, then the next, Claire's curly head popped up, and she waved at me. Hello or good-bye, I didn't know, and it didn't matter. That wave, that smile, filled me with hope. I might be able to drive that clacking darkness back to hell after all.

It was like I had just made a *second* person reappear.

AFTER WE LEFT COFFEE INVASION, Ziggy saw me to my car, pounded the roof, and said, "Take care, Noah. I'll see you soon."

I still had questions for Ziggy, such as who he really was, and how the hell I was supposed to save the city from the evil brewing in the PfefferBrau Haus. But I realized I didn't need to know everything all at once. There was something about Ziggy that went deeper than the perfect hair and the expensive suit. I trusted him.

He'd only said "Take care" to me once, but it was as though he was always taking care of me. First by finding my car that night Evan was so sick, then by helping me convince Jaime to come back to me, and tonight by saving me from the Marr—helping me name my enemy and showing me the next step to defeating it.

It was almost as though he were acting like a father. A good one.

Not that I'd know what that was like.

I hadn't seen my own father in years.

Good riddance.

My dad was an alcoholic. Big deal, right? Most alcoholics I know get straight to it with Wild Turkey or Jim Beam. But not Dear Old Dad. His poison of choice was—you guessed it—PfefferBrau Porter. The kind Sherell Wexler was found in.

And man, did it take him a long time to get wasted on beer. But he managed it almost every night, and by the time he was thirty-five, he had the gut to prove it.

When he wasn't at home knocking me around, he worked for the paper company. He had definite opinions about clear-cutting ("You like books, don'tcha? You can't make omelets without breaking a few eggs") and woodland species protected by the Forest Service ("Shoot all those damn spotted owls, let God sort 'em out"). And I agreed with all of them. Especially when he took off his John Deere cap and showed that full head of brindled hair, just like Pfeffer's. That hair carried power.

I was too little to remember the first thing I did that pissed him off. But I do remember the look in his eye and the close-up of the fridge before he slammed my face into it.

I remember Mom cradling me in her lap as I cried. I remember her trying to calm me down, all the while telling me she couldn't take me to a doctor because they'd ask questions. I remember her saying, "It's not you, honey. Daddy's just had a bad day at work, that's all."

All I understood was the hurt. I remember Dad calling up from the basement where he was drinking Pfeffer-Brau Porters, one after the other, watching a Trail Blazers game on the black-and-white TV with the rabbit ears and the faux wood paneling. "Shut him up, Eileen. Shut him up or I'll shut him up."

And even though I didn't really understand what was going on, I found a way to keep quiet. *That* time.

The times when I wouldn't stop crying, Mom piled Cilla and me into the back of the Buick station wagon, which smelled of cherry air fresheners. She would drive us around and tell us stories about what Dad was like before he dropped out of high school. She talked about how charming he could be. She called him a real catch, but even then I knew she wasn't trying to convince *us*.

By the time I got to grade school, we had a whole new set of problems. The main one being, how did we hide what Dad imprinted on my face, or on my arms? No one at school understood how I kept getting black eyes. Playing basketball, I said. Ran into backboards. Did a face-plant on my front drive.

The kids and the teachers might've understood me getting backhanded now and then. I could be a handful.

I probably deserved it. But nobody would've ever understood this part: I *liked* the pain. It was a sign to me that, yeah, I'd fucked up, but it was all over now, right, son? Ready to start again?

Without that pain, and a mark I wore until it faded or the cast came off, I would've always been under someone's boot heel, a fuckup without the possibility of parole, the kid who never did anything right.

Evan understood what was really going on, but he never said it to my face. I'd show up to school with a broken clavicle (skiing, I said, even though everyone knew I didn't ski), and he'd say, "Let's play at my house today, Noah." And we'd get to his house and play Pong on his Atari, and then his mom with the butt-length brown hair would invite me to stay for dinner, which I always did. Then, if it wasn't a school night, Ev and I would watch an old movie on his Betamax. It was always the kind of movie with a manageable scare, like *The Blob* or *Creature from the Black Lagoon*, where the threat was just some cheesy special effect—a guy in a diving suit, soft candle wax to stand in for dripping flesh.

If it *was* a school night, Evan's dad, Dr. Tillstrom, would keep looking at his watch at the dinner table, and sometime over dessert (chocolate pudding, or tapioca with raspberry jam), he'd say, "I think we're okay now, Noah." Meaning: Your dad's probably passed out in front of the Blazers game. It's okay for you to sneak home.

· · ·

And then came the night my dad ran away the *first* time.
I was ten years old. Dad had just come back from a weekend hunting in the woods with the boys. He rarely came
home with any trophies. His breath always smelled like
beer.

But this trip was different. I'd heard his truck pull up in
the drive and, instead of rushing out to greet him, I pulled
the covers tighter over my head. Even then, I knew I was
more likely to get Nice Dad if I waited until morning.

My parents were having a fight, and I closed my bedroom door to muffle the yelling.

They were in the basement. The screaming wasn't
unusual. What was unusual was that it was my mom's
voice that was raised. Then Dad barked, "For god's sake,
Eileen, keep it down! You'll wake the kids!"

"You knew! I told you when you brought the last one
home I wouldn't be carving up any animals!"

"Well, the rules have changed, princess. And if you
want to stay with me, I suggest you change with them."

"Not this time, Tray. Get that thing out of my driveway."

"*My* driveway. I pay the bills."

"We both pay the bills."

There was a silence. And in that silence, the door to
our Jack and Jill bathroom creaked open and Cilla, thir-
teen years old, wearing a roller-disco pajama ensemble,
came creeping in. I scooted to the far side of the bed. She

climbed in next to me, wrapping me tightly, keeping me safe.

"What are they arguing about this time?" I whispered.

"I don't know. But I don't like it. It feels different."

I didn't need her to tell me. Even there in the dark, the two of us coiled up to hide from the world, the air felt taut, like a guitar string about to snap.

Dad started up again. "I don't see what the problem is. You buy steak shrink-wrapped at the meat counter."

"The difference is I don't have to cut anything's head off or scoop out its intestines."

"What do you think sausage comes in, princess?"

"I'm not doing it, Tray."

"Four fucking hours, Eileen. That's how long I waited in the freezing cold in that stupid blind. I bagged it fair and square. That kill will feed us for a month."

"I DON'T GIVE A CARE!"

I don't know what set Dad off, but it was probably the phrase "give a care," which struck him as too stupid to be taken seriously. He went off on a laughing jag. He chortled like a Santa, only a mean one. It was a laugh that said, *I own you. I own everything.* Then there was the sound of a slap, and it didn't sound hard enough to have come from Dad, who usually put more oomph behind his shots.

Oh shit, please *tell me Mom didn't fight back.* But she had, because that mean-Santa laugh stopped, then there was a scuffle, a clunk, and the shrill note of a piano key sticking.

I closed my eyes. "She's caught a corner," I whispered. Cilla and I both knew what that looked like. Carpets weren't so bad. A fridge straight-on wasn't so bad. It was the sharp edges, like the ones on a coffee table or a piano, that did the most damage.

There was a wail, a sob that was more than a sob. The front door slammed. I heard a thud out on the front lawn, then Dad yelling, "I killed it, you can damn well clean it!"

Mom was on the front porch now, yelling, "I'm sorry! Come back! Please come back!"

Jesus Christ, let him go, I thought. And in that darkness, Cilla took a hand out from around me and ran it through my hair, her cool fingertips coaxing waves out of all that roughness, and it felt to me just like a backbeat.

She opened her mouth and began to sing. "Blackbird singing in the dead of night . . ." And it was so sweet and so soft, just the same line from that Beatles song over and over, nowhere near on-key, but the sound of her voice was enough. I was surrounded by sweet music. We were going to be okay.

The next morning when we woke up, Mom was sporting seven stitches on her left temple and there was a deer carcass on the front lawn. Dad had gone but left his kill. To prove a point, probably. He was always one for big, bloody gestures. But this was gruesome even for him.

I want to say that thing on the lawn didn't look like a

deer anymore, but it did. The antlers were magnificent. Prince Fucking Bambi. But the stillness was creepy. The thing's eyes were open and glassy, and lower down was the worst: Its haunch was a bloody mess full of buckshot and exposed muscle. It looked like some really twisted Christmas decoration.

And here was the thing: Mom didn't even seem to notice it. She drank her instant coffee, kissed us both good-bye, told us to have a good day at school, and drove off to work at her accounting firm. Cilla and I stared at the deer for a long time, then I told her to go too. She was shaking too hard. She was no help.

After she left, I tried to haul the thing off on my own, but it was so heavy I only got as far as the curb.

And that was the first time I called Evan and said, "I need help moving a body."

It was spitting rain out.

Between the two of us slinging that thing in a picnic blanket, we managed to get up the cul-de-sac, even though after two seconds we were soaked, and blood (not ours) ran into the gutters. A bunch of living room curtains pulled back and faces stared at us from warm homes, but no one came out.

Working together, Evan and I made it to the Finkbeiners', through their backyard, and into the ravine, where we found a patch of ground that wasn't pitted with too many fir tree roots. We buried Prince Bambi. Evan cracked a joke about the whole experience turning him into a vegetarian, but we both knew he didn't mean it. Nobody we knew was a vegetarian. Only sissies, which we definitely were not. Not that day, at least. We were fucking cavemen.

Finally, after an hour, we threw the last muddy shovelful of dirt on the mound and leaned back. Our hands were blistered from the shovels and we were soaked from the rain, our shoulders torqued from all the hoisting and dragging.

Only then, when the work was done, did I start crying. I couldn't get over it, how one minute that royal thing would be browsing around some forest, nosing a piece of loose bark, and the next, dying a sudden and painful death. It seemed to me that I could feel its fear and pain and confusion. *Why is this happening to me? What did I do to deserve this?*

Ev didn't put his arm around me or anything like that. Just stood by my side, popping the blisters on his hands, the ones in the valley between his thumb and forefinger.

Finally I wiped my eyes and said, "Do you think it was quick?"

He stared at me then. Long and hard. Finally he said, "Noah, that deer didn't even know he was a victim."

I DIDN'T GET A CHANCE TO TALK TO EV the next day until personal finance. He sat behind me, munching chocolate-covered espresso beans (don't ask me where he got them), and whispered, "What happened to your head?"

I thought no one would notice. I deliberately hadn't spiked my mohawk, hoping the green in my hair would hide the green and purple in my skin from where I'd landed on the speed bump escaping the Marr behind Cinema 21.

But of course he knew I was injured. He always knew.

"Mosh pit accident," I said.

"Gentlemen. We've talked about this," Mr. Eizenzimmer said to us from the front of the class, where he was droning on about entering checks in your register before writing the actual check. "If I hear one more disruption from you I'll have to put you on different sides of the room." We never paid attention to Mr. Eizenzimmer because he never did more than threaten. Plus he had a face like a ferret and wore the same brown cords every day.

So as soon as his back was turned, Evan slipped me some of his espresso beans. He probably thought they'd help my head. An instant later he lobbed me a note on ruled paper, with tabs still on the edges from where it had been ripped out of a notebook. It read: *Don't freak. Sonia wants to pull out.*

Great. I suppose I couldn't blame her, but now that I'd seen the Marr, I knew what was at stake. If we didn't do anything, it was probably only a matter of time before she became just another face in its black abyss.

I started scribbling a note back to Ev, but before I got a couple of words down, he lobbed another one in my lap. *Don't even think about it. I'll talk to Sonia. You start composing.*

That day, while Ev worked on the Old Girls, Crock was looking for a practice space. The three of us caught up in the stairwell behind the speech classroom after school. We usually hung out there because nobody ever used it. Hidden in plain sight and all that.

Crock was carrying a flip pad and had a pencil behind his ear. I hadn't seen this version of Crock in months—the one who wasn't barfing in my car or picking up leather-skinned divorcées.

"Can't practice in my garage," he said. "I asked. Idiot Willy is like your sister—he sleeps during the day. *And* he has a gun. We can't do it at Sonia's, because it will disrupt her mother's Bridge Club routine, and we can't do it at Jaime's or Ev's, because their parents think you're a bad influence."

I tried not to take it personally, especially since they used to have me over all the time.

"It's the mohawk, Noah. That's all it is. About the hair."

But he was trying too hard. There was some other, newer reason they didn't want Evan hanging out with me anymore, but I didn't have time to worry about that now.

I nodded. Fair enough.

"What about the band room here at school?" Evan asked.

"Tried that," Crock said. "Turns out the band geeks need it. They're rehearsing some shit about princesses. Supposed to be funny."

I knew what he was talking about because we'd all seen the posters in the music wing. *Once Upon a Mattress.* The spring musical. So what if it was funny. We still needed a rehearsal space. So Crock and Ev and I did what we always did when we didn't know what to do.

We went record shopping.

Like a lot of places in Portland, Jojo's Records had a former life as something grand, maybe a ballroom. The ceiling was so tall it might as well have been in space, and there were all these curlicued things painted right on it: fat cherubs and shepherdesses and stuff like that. There was a huge water stain above Soundtracks, which sometimes dripped big fat drops of rain mixed with sewage from the plumbing upstairs. Evan said it wasn't much of a loss. He said that even if there was a flood and it took out the whole Soundtracks section along with Country Western, no one would cry any tears. Except maybe the Country Western people. But they cried over everything, so it didn't count.

Of course, since it was Jojo's, the walls up to those gods and cherubs and shepherdesses were papered with rock posters. The Pretenders, the Rolling Stones, the Clash, the Who, the Beatles. Bowie was there too, in his different incarnations: Aladdin Sane with that blindingly red hair and red lightning bolt on his face, the Thin White Duke looking cruel and sexy, the Scary Monster smoking a cigarette in a Harlequin getup.

And then there was my incarnation of Bowie—the suave guy in the expensive suits with the bright yellow hair. There were Bowie bumper stickers, Bowie bobble-heads, Bowie stand-ups. I didn't blame Jojo for all the swag. Bowie was big. Jojo had to make money.

We had to step over the drunk in the tinfoil hat to get into the store.

There was the usual tinkle of bells above the door

when Crock and Ev and I walked in and inhaled that musty record store smell. Jojo was standing alone behind the front case, reading a copy of *Willamette Week*, the alternative Portland newspaper.

Behind him, lined up under a long row of windowsills, leaned pictures of the Disappearing Girls—black-and-white flyers pasted to pieces of cardboard, a candle sitting in the window above each. Probably a fire hazard, but it was a nice touch—a beacon for every girl to come home.

Crock skulked off toward the cassettes, which fit in his jeans pockets more easily than LPs. He liked getting things but not paying for them.

I said that, free or not, cassettes weren't worth crap. LPs were the only thing—even scratched. I loved the shine and groove of vinyl. And Jojo had bins full, new and glossy or used and worn. The really valuable records, like the bootlegs, were in clear plastic slipcases that folded over like giant sandwich baggies.

"Hey, Jojo," I said.

Jojo looked up. He had these freakishly huge eyes, like a praying kitten. And this stringy gray hair that ran halfway down his back. He said he used to be a roadie, mainly for Jefferson Airplane, but we weren't sure that was real. Not that he was lying—he probably had really convincing LSD flashbacks.

"Hey, Noah," he said. "What happened to you, man? That's an impressive goose egg on your head. Plus your aura's all wonky. Whoa, look at all those colors. It's psy-chedelic."

"Stage-diving accident," I mumbled.

Jojo folded up his paper. "I don't mean to get all paren-tal on you and shit, but if I were you I'd at least take the safety pin out of your nose before going out slam danc-ing. That could do some serious damage."

I suppose it was nice of him to show an interest, but we came here to forget about me. At least for a little while. "Are you alone, Jojo? Where's Derek?" Jojo had great taste in records but lousy taste in employees. They were all skate punks named Derek or Dennis. All of them robbed him blind.

"You mean Darlene? She took off, man. I put her on a train to San Francisco. She's going to dance school."

"What kind of dance?" Evan asked.

"Exotic," Jojo said. "She says even sleazeballs pay better than me."

"Did she have a snake?" Crock said. How he heard the words "exotic dancer" from the other side of the store, I'll never know.

"I didn't see one, man," Jojo said. He stared blankly at a spot just above my head, probably looking for a snake that wasn't there.

Talk about lost in space. Ground control to Jojo.

"Are you okay here on your own?" I asked. I counted three guys with duffel bags who were about to walk off with everything in the "B" bins.

Jojo said, "Oh yeah. No problem. Except I've gotta pee. And I don't think I've eaten since Friday."

It was now Monday. He'd probably eaten, just forgotten about it. Still, there was a pulling at the pit of my stomach like I felt when Evan needed help. "Why don't you take a bathroom break, Jojo? Let us watch the counter for a sec."

"Really? You'd do that for me?" Jojo said, his eyes suddenly focusing.

"You need to pee, right?"

"It's okay, man, I've been doing it in this Big Gulp." He picked up a giant waxy container from the windowsill and shook it. It sloshed and smelled like ammonia. "But you know what? I could use a pizza. Why don't you and Evan watch the counter? It's real easy. All you have to do is make change. But do me a favor, will ya? Keep Crock away from the till."

"No prob," Evan said. "Crock has work to do. Don't you, Crock?"

Crock had been subtly picking at the lock on the cassette case with no luck.

"I do?" he said, trying to look innocent.

"Yesssss," I said extra slow. "You have to go to the PfefferBrau Haus and enter us in the contest. You're our manager, remember?"

His eyes popped open. "Oh yeah," he said. "Work. I'll get right on it."

He left the store with a jangle of the bells.

After he left, Evan stared after him. Finally he said, "Huh. Jaime thinks that guy is her prince."

I'd forgotten that little factoid. But Ev was right. One of life's great mysteries. Jaime acted all goofy around Crock and blushed when he even said hi to her. And she was supposed to be smart. Why couldn't she see the guy was a major hound? There was no way the two of them would ever be a couple. She wanted a boyfriend; Crock just wanted sex. Lots of it. With different women. True, Jaime was female so there was a good chance they might hook up, but then Crock would ignore her afterward.

So Ev and I invoked the "hands off the Old Girls" rule. We put ourselves between them at parties. We suggested Crock might have better luck with someone sluttier.

Jojo seemed to know what we were thinking, about how even smart girls could be turned into complete ditzes. "It's the chest hair, man. Makes 'em all stupid. Girls, I mean," Jojo said.

Ev and I both looked down at our chests. Pitiful. I was pale as a ghost and Ev was worse than me, what with being scrawny and having a giant scar on his rib cage from his appendectomy.

Working for Jojo wasn't hard. I stood at the door and asked people leaving to open their gym bags and back-packs, which seemed to be what Jojo needed most. I busted four kids, and none of them put up a fight. They seemed thankful I didn't call the police.

When Jojo had been gone an hour, there was a lull in business. "Not bad," Evan said.

I had no idea what he was talking about. "What's not bad?"

"That tune you're humming."

I hadn't even realized I'd been doing it aloud, but that was Evan for you. Keyed into what I was thinking before I even thought it.

"Nothing," I said, and sang the chorus of "Smoking Ruin," the song that had been running through my head since last night.

Nothing breaks over me
Nothing gives me hope
Nothing hit me with a great black claw
I'd be a smoking ruin but there's nothing left to smoke

When I was done, Ev said, "Wow. Perky."

He was right. Who would pay money to listen to such morbid crap?

Then Ev went on, "You know what would sound really good under that?" And he started a low rumbling counterpoint. He wasn't humming exactly. The sounds he made came out more like *now now now*. He picked at his left thigh as though it were terraced with strings.

And that was how Jojo found us when he came back at closing time, carrying a pizza box. It was so greasy you could see the shape of the disc under the square cardboard.

I was mumbling lyrics, Evan was muttering *now now now*.

"Hey, man. That sounds pretty good. You should put some instruments to that. I think there are some in the Maxi Pad. Come on, I'll show you."

Now, okay, Ev and I had only partly been paying attention to his customers, so maybe Jojo was trying to punish us in a really disgusting way we didn't understand. The Maxi Pad? Seriously? What kind of bloody torture was that? Did it even exist? Or was it like Darlene's snake or his career with Jefferson Airplane?

Jojo saw us silently trying to puzzle it out, and said, "Oh yeah." He pulled a checkbook from a drawer under the till and wrote out two checks for twenty-five dollars apiece. He handed one to each of us, then picked up the pizza box he'd been carrying. "You can work Saturdays, right? Hey, I hope you guys like garlic. I had them put on extra. Goes over real well with the ladies." He breathed on us. "Just playin' with you guys. Seriously. You two need to lighten up."

He smiled and rattled a couple of keys on a ring attached to his belt. He unlocked a door I'd never seen at the back of the store.

I could tell from Evan's look that he didn't want to follow him. He mouthed the words *Maxi Pad?* to me. But I was in a zone where, if someone opened a door for me, goddamn it, I was going to go through.

Jojo led us up a wooden staircase that was worn in the middle and smelled like cat pee. I'd never been upstairs before, but I knew there had to be one, even with the high ceilings on the store below. If you looked at the building from the outside you could see three levels of windows before the crumbling cornices of the rooftop. There were even these weird gargoyles, faces that seemed human but with expressions that looked like they all had really bad toothaches.

Inside, we stopped at the first landing. There was another set of stairs going up—presumably to the space with the cornices and the toothache gargoyles, but this was our destination.

Jojo took out his keys, unlocked a door with a frosted pane, walked in, and flicked a switch.

The lights went up on the next stage of our lives.

"MAKE YOURSELVES AT HOME," JOJO SAID, clearing dirty laundry off a futon and dumping heaps of tie-dyed shirts onto his white shag carpet, which looked like the hide of an albino yak. This place was huge. I could see why he called it the Maxi Pad. Everything about it was maxi. There weren't any rooms—only glass bricks marking off space, making it look like a warehouse-sized aquarium.

Ev lost no time worshipping at the shrine of Jojo's instruments. "Oh my god! Is that a Rickenbacker 4001 JG?" Ev grabbed a bass, its body shaped like the letter *V* with mother-of-pearl inlay.

There were stands with rows and rows of basses and guitars, plus something under a thick linty blanket that took up so much room it had to be a drum kit. At least twelve pieces. Sonia would go apeshit.

Then there were the pictures lining the walls. A much

younger Jojo with Grace Slick of Jefferson Airplane. Jojo with Beat poet Allen Ginsberg. Jojo with Jimi Hendrix. Jojo with the hedonistic drummer of the Who, Keith Moon. Jojo with Paul McCartney.

So he hadn't made up his past after all. If anything, he'd left a lot out.

"Wow. Could we use your space sometime? We're trying to put together a demo for the PfefferFest."

Jojo flipped the lid on the pizza box and helped himself to a slice, which he ate standing up, grease dripping down his chin.

"I don't know, man," Jojo said. "I mean, someone should use this stuff. But the PfefferFest? I know hate isn't healthy, but that place is just evil. Why not start someplace smaller? Maybe open mic night at the Long Goodbye?"

"It has to be the PfefferFest."

"Why?"

Evan stared extra hard at me, as though *I* were the one being eaten inside out by the black plague.

I blurted, "Because of the money. Our drummer has this crazy idea about going to college."

"Oh, right. I forgot about the purse." Jojo scratched his head. "And hey, the Pfeffer guys were acquitted and everybody deserves a second chance . . ."

"Even cannibals," Evan muttered.

". . . but I don't like that one dude. You know, with the hair? He reminds me of these guys I knew in the Haight."

He chuckled. "Good times, man, good times. You know, before they got blown to bits in 'Nam." He stared overlong at his dining room table, which, like Jojo himself, was old enough to be retro but not old enough to be antique. He seemed mesmerized by the flicker of the mica in the plastic surface. "What were we talking about again? Oh yeah, food." He pointed to the pizza box. "Dig in, everybody."

Ev and I tore ourselves away from the Museum of Rock Art and sat down for a slice with our new boss.

"So, it's just you two? Are you putting together an acoustic set or what?"

Evan said, "Nah. We've got a drummer and this girl on keys."

"You're bringing a lady around?" Jojo said.

"Two. The drummer's a girl."

He practically jumped out of his chair. "Oh, crap. We'd better get busy." He rummaged in a pants pocket and pulled out a pair of greasy twenty-dollar bills, then handed them to me. "Get us some cleaning stuff, will ya? There's a Safeway down the street. Wait, you know what to get, right? To clean, like, furniture and shit?"

Across the room, Evan sank heavily into his own bones, which seemed so thin and brittle through his T-shirt I was afraid they might break into plaster and rain down on Country Western in the store below. "Yes, Noah knows," he said. "We both do."

• • •

I couldn't wait to tell the Old Girls about the Maxi Pad. Sonia would go crazy over that drum kit, and then she'd have to come back to me.

Us. Come back to *us.*

The next day I caught up with them in the hall between third and fourth periods. Or almost caught up with them. You couldn't mistake those heads of hair.

I racewalked to catch up. I was reaching out to tap Sonia on the shoulder when I heard her say, "Yeah, well, that's the problem. He can come through *sometimes.*"

I was left there with one hand out. I felt my reaching fingers turn to Jell-O.

I ghosted them, following two paces behind.

"Look. I'm not saying you need to trust him again," Jaime said. "I know what he put you through. I'm just saying—"

"It's different for you," Sonia cut her off. "You don't need this. I do. I want the money."

"I'm trying to tell you I don't think it's a game to Noah either. He's different. It scares me." She leaned in close, but even though she whispered, I heard her under the giggles and scoffs of five hundred other between-classes kids. "Have you met Ziggy yet?"

Every nerve in my body tingled and thrummed. I swept along behind them, hardly daring to breathe.

I didn't hear what Sonia replied, but then Jaime said, "Well, I have. It was creepy. I mean, he said all the right things, but still . . . it reminded me of Noah's father."

In the halls of Gresham High, which smelled of sweat and hair spray and Pine-Sol, the warning bell rang. I nearly dropped my books. My head was so thick and brittle it felt like it was stuffed with straw.

No one was supposed to talk about my dad. Nobody. That was the deal. Especially for the ones who knew what really happened.

Now, between classes, the pressure in my head was so bad I screamed to pour off some of the pain, but no one around me noticed, so maybe I didn't make a sound.

But everybody noticed the next part, when I sprinted up between the girls and knocked the books out of Jaime's hand. "Bitch," I spat.

It didn't make me feel any better. I might as well have kicked her down a flight of stairs.

Oh god, the shame. No no no. This was all wrong. I was a good guy. I wasn't my father.

I put my head down and charged away from them, around the corner, and into chem lab.

Something else must've taken hold of me.

I braced myself against the doorframe of chem lab. The halls were almost empty now; most of the other kids were where they needed to go. One or two were sprinting down the hall, trailing dust devils of notebook paper and color-coded subject folders. And that was when I felt the chill.

It wasn't coming from chem but somewhere else. Everywhere and nowhere all at once. A soul-sucking chill. Roiling clouds of black smoke came in through the window. The metallic tang of blood coming with it.

Noah, it whispered. *You really thought you could lose me?*

I knew that voice. I'd heard it Sunday night, taunting me, goading me with grimaces of half-digested faces.

Inside the classroom, Mr. Arepedian was handing a beaker to Tyler Eubanks. He looked up, his gray comb-over flopping on top of a shiny brown skull. "Are you okay, Noah?"

Yes, Noah, the Marr hissed, reaching its black lobster claws for me. *Are you okay? Or should I tell you how I cut up the girls before I buried them? Or how I'm going to feed on your friend Evan until there's nothing left?*

I backed out of chem class and stared down the hall.

It was coming for me.

I felt a tap on my shoulder.

I wheeled around.

If I thought Sonia was crazy-mad when she slammed my fingers in the car door, it was nothing compared to the way she looked now. She was dripping acid. Her eyes were like death rays.

She brought her knee up right between my legs. Hard.

I doubled over. The pain was so bad I couldn't breathe.

Yesssss, the cloud hissed. *Deliciousss . . .*

I tried to crawl away but was blocked in every direction by a thousand pairs of feet. The whole school was looking down at me, nobody helping.

One of them kicked me over onto my back. I looked up. Sonia planted one black boot on my chest, bent over, grabbed hold of the safety pin in my left nostril, and yanked.

IT'S NOT EASY TO TEAR THROUGH CARTILAGE.

Sonia took a long time to pull that hardware out of my nose. She braced herself against me. She grimaced as she ripped me in two.

And I let her.

I wasn't tough about it either. I screamed and screamed and I didn't care who heard me.

I was rolling on the floor and my face was a red sea, deep and parted. And I saw her, standing above me, holding a safety pin in her right hand, blood cascading down her arm. So help me, she was *smirking*.

Delicious. It's even better when it's from someone you love, the Marr said, as the black, sucking void drew nearer.

I tried to talk but could only gurgle. Could nobody see this thing? Ziggy had said I was more sensitive to it, but could no one else feel the cold? See the swirling black-ness? Hear the screams of the half digested?

I didn't see Evan before he smothered my face. "Here, hold this," he said, shoving a piece of checked purple material over my nose. He hoisted me to my feet. He put my free arm around his shoulder. He was so skinny his body felt like kindling. "Time to go, man," he said. And then he shouted over his shoulder to Sonia (I guessed), "I don't care what kind of daddy issues you've got, but you've got no right—"

"I have every right! He called Jaime a bitch!"

"Don't you have any idea what you've done? Swear to god, I'm making sure Noah sues your ass *and* your dad-dy's ass, you twisted fuck. Kiss college good-bye."

I wasn't so out of my head that I didn't realize that that was the worst threat he could have made.

And he wasn't done yet. Evan turned to look at the congregation of teenage gawkers. They weren't look-ing at me with my fucked-up face. They were looking at Sonia and her bloody arm in a way that made *freak* take on a whole new meaning.

The Marr was right behind Evan, reaching for his dreads.

He didn't even see it.

"And to the rest of you assholes, thanks for helping!" he said—*spat*—and flipped everyone off. Everyone in the whole school.

Ev dragged me down the hall and out the door, where

a Volkswagen Rabbit was idling in a No Parking zone. Jaime was behind the wheel. Evan opened the back of the Rabbit and shoved me in.

"Can you park here?" I said, or tried to say. It came out a salty gurgle.

Ev climbed into the shotgun seat and slammed the door behind him. "Go go go!"

Jaime gunned the engine and peeled out of the parking lot. She honked a lot. She probably didn't check her mirrors.

I stared at her back. That was a lot of skin, and thin pink straps that looked too delicate to be a swimming suit. "Is that your bra? Where's your shirt?"

"It's wrapped around your face, doofus," Evan said.

And even though the whole world was throbbing, I smiled. Evan used my pain to get a girl to strip. "Nice one," I said.

"Shut up," Jaime said. "And lie on your side so you don't choke."

I did what she said, and pretty soon there was a flood of red pooling on the upholstery.

"I'm getting your . . ."

"Left left LEFT!" Ev yelled.

Jaime made a sharp turn and my head hurled against the side door. I didn't feel a thing.

"Bleach won't work on this," I said, looking at the red pool under my head. "It'll discolor—"

"Get him to shut up," Jaime spat.

"Shut up," Evan said.

I heard the squeal of the brakes, smelled the burn of the rubber. We spun a doughnut and landed in front of Gresham Urgent Care. Then Ev leapt out and hauled my arm over his shoulder. My last sight before being manhandled into triage was of him and Jaime standing shoulder to shoulder. Jaime in a bra and miniskirt.

In the exam room, a nurse poked my arm with something that was painful enough to make every pore in my body break out in a sweat. She ran a tube from my elbow to something hanging above my head.

Evan's dad, Dr. Tillstrom, came in, snapping on rubber gloves. He was a tall, lurching guy with receding blond hair. He wore glasses with little magnifiers on them. They made him look like a giant insect, his hands mandibles as they counted sharp tools on a tray. He sat on a rolling stool and skidded over to me.

"What did you do?" Dr. Tillstrom said. I honestly didn't know. But it had to be something, didn't it? I always deserved *something*.

He went on: "Whatever you're into, you'd better be keeping my son out of it *this time*." He lifted Jaime's shirt from my face and nodded to a nurse, who started dabbing.

"I should let you stay awake for this 'cause it's gonna hurt, and I think someone should teach you a lesson. Lucky for you I've had my fill of watching young boys in pain." Dr. Tillstrom nodded again to the nurse, who found a port in the hose going into my arm and stuck a syringe of thick clear liquid in it.

I felt a cool tingling all over my body. It only lasted a second.

Then I didn't feel anything at all.

The next thing I knew I was standing in the corner of the room, watching Dr. Tillstrom bark at a nurse about lost tissue. It wasn't just that I'd stood up from where I was and walked over to the corner. I was standing there *and* I was on the exam table at the same time. Two places at once.

I watched myself lying there. I saw the soles of my boots. I saw my hands tremor and shake as Dr. Tillstrom did something to my face, which was buried somewhere under a paper sheet. I wondered what the whole kerfuffle was about. Why was that poor kid so traumatized?

That Noah didn't hear Dr. Tillstrom say, "It's all right. You're going to be okay."

That Noah didn't see Dr. Tillstrom raise his glasses and wipe something from an eye with his shirtsleeve.

He stood up and flung some instrument into a biohazard sink. "I can't do this," he said to his nurse. "He's too much like my own boy. Get Lewiston in here. I'll take Dementia Woman next door."

Dr. Tillstrom snapped off his gloves, ripped the scrubs from his body, and lurched out of the room.

I watched the Noah on the exam table relax. And why

not? If pain meant forgiveness, this had to be worth multiple lifetimes of screwups.

I don't know how long I stood in the corner watching someone (Lewiston?) stitch up the poor idiot on the table before I realized I wasn't alone. Something was brushing my shoulders. Lightly. Like down feathers. They were so gentle, so warm.

I didn't need to look to know that Ziggy was standing by my side.

"How long have you been watching over me?" I said.

"Today? Not long."

I remembered the night in Coffee Invasion, when Ziggy had said that the Marr could have half-digested Evan, but a part of him could still be safe at home.

"Did it get me? Am I going to start disappearing?"

Ziggy shook his head sadly. "No, lad. You get to stay. I don't know if it's a blessing or not."

Together, we watched Lewiston sew up my nose. Clear liquid dripped from a bag that hung above my body through a tube that ran into my left elbow.

Still didn't feel a thing.

"You know this isn't as bad as it gets. There's much worse ahead," Ziggy said. His voice made doom sound like a song.

I remembered Dr. Tillstrom throwing his instrument in the sink, saying, "I can't do this. He's too much like my own boy."

"I know," I told Ziggy now. "I don't like to think about it."

"You're safe here. For the moment at least," he said. "Go ahead and let yourself think."

And I did. I let it all wash over me. What I knew was happening and what was about to happen. I knew what was coming wouldn't be as fast as tearing my nose. It would creep and retreat, creep and retreat. Some days I'd feel like we were winning, but we wouldn't in the end.

There. I admitted it.

Ziggy wasn't here to sing—he was here to help us let go.

As soon as I understood that, it didn't matter so much. And I understood more about what was important.

Images came back to me in reverse. First of all, there was Jaime in her bra and miniskirt. I suppose that should've shocked me, seeing her half-dressed. But the impressive part was that she had actually given me the shirt off her back.

I was pretty sure *that woman* wouldn't have approved, but Jay did it anyway.

Then there was the way Crock was completely useless until something needed organizing.

I thought about Sonia's rattail of a braid, and the way it smacked me across the nose when we made out. Being with her was worth every mark on my body.

I remembered a much younger Cilla, who, before she started calling me nimrod, had hummed me to sleep when our parents fought. I remember how, even though she couldn't carry a tune, she'd made music that drove back the night.

And I remembered Evan. Hoisting me to my feet, dragging me to a No Parking zone when he looked like he didn't have the strength to drag a hamster. The way he'd flipped off everyone in the entire school and told Sonia I was suing her ass—which, by the way, I had no intention of doing.

Then I remembered Evan the way he used to be, before his appendectomy, before everything about him filled me with dread, starting with his hair. He used to be a good-looking kid. When the two of us stood side by side, you could hear the girls whisper, "Evan's going to be the heartbreaker." And I wasn't ticked off, because I knew it was true. All that silky blond hair, cheekbones so high they looked like bookshelves, his lopsided smile that made it seem he was flirting even when he wasn't.

I remembered the two of us playing Mafia in seventh grade, and Evan undoing all the damage I'd done.

He was always undoing my damage.

"What's happening?" the nurse asked Dr. Lewiston, from what seemed like miles away.

"It looks like he's crying," Dr. Lewiston said. "Up the sedation. This isn't supposed to hurt." The nurse found a fat syringe and emptied it into the tube in my arm.

I felt a tugging in my gut. I was going back and I didn't want to. I wanted to stay there, with Ziggy. That pain belonged to some other kid, the one with the fucked-up face.

I grabbed Ziggy's forearm. I felt the soft material of his suit. "Promise me you'll stay with me through the worst of it. Promise you won't leave."

The tugging in my gut got harder.

I looked at Ziggy, waiting for him to say something. But he never did. Instead, he showed me what I knew had been there all along.

Wings. Giant golden wings sprouting from the back of his perfect golden suit. They twinkled in the light—even here in this room where the overheads were so harsh and blue they hummed.

Ziggy looked so perfect, so unmarred, he might as well have been painted on Jojo's ceiling.

The tugging got harder.

"Help me," I begged him. "I'm going to fall."

All Ziggy could do was watch.

11

"HE'S COMING AROUND," I HEARD.

I looked up. I saw crappy acoustic tiles. Watermarks. Humming fluorescent lights. I was on the exam table.

I lifted my head and tried to see into the upper corner of the room. I was looking for something, but I didn't know what.

"Easy, son," Dr. Tillstrom said. He was looking at something on a chart. His mask was gone. No insect glasses. No sharp tools.

Hadn't he pulled some kind of switcheroo on me? Traded me to another doctor? It seemed like he had, but I couldn't remember that either.

It didn't matter. He was here now.

I looked at the upper corner again. I was convinced something important had just happened. I could hear it,

I could feel it, but I couldn't quite remember it.

"Was Ziggy here?" I mumbled.

"Ziggy?" he looked at his nurse. "Not that I know of, son. But there's a collection of people in the waiting room for you. Evan. Jaime. Your mom. Cilla. Sonia. Sonia's dad. Sonia's dad's attorney."

I gently touched my face. I felt gauze, and smooth tape that stretched from cheek to cheek. And underneath, lips. Stubble growing on my chin, but a gaping abyss where my nose used to be.

"Can't feel my nose."

"Don't worry. It's still there. We numbed it up a bit, is all. I think you'll be pleased with the scar. And if you're not, you can always use makeup. I'm sure your sister has plenty to spare."

He was joking, but he was working too hard at it. The left side of his face sagged.

I'd lost count of the number of times Dr. Tillstrom had fixed me up. This one seemed to have wrecked him in some way. I could see it in the stoop in his back, the circles under his eyes.

He knew something important. Something that I was supposed to remember, but I couldn't.

He made a note on a chart. "Have you considered pressing charges?"

"Against who?"

"Sonia. Evan and Jaime told me all about it. I don't

think anyone would blame you if you want to put that girl in McLaren. The whole school saw what she did. You have plenty of witnesses."

"You mean juvie? Sonia doesn't belong in juvie."

"She belongs somewhere, son. What she did to you was no accident."

"It wasn't like that. I called Jaime a bitch. I deserved this."

He pointed a finger at me. He seemed happy to be in parent mode again. "That's your father talking. You deserved nothing."

"But why? How can you be so sure?"

He seemed to consider this. Then he sat on his rolling chair and scooted over to me. "Earlier today, when Sonia was ripping up your face, did you defend yourself? Try to hit back?"

I didn't say anything. What could I say? I remembered looking up at her smirk, her bloody hand, like a horror film.

Dr. Tillstrom found something in my expression that satisfied him. "I didn't think so. You never do. Unless you're defending someone else."

I didn't tell him about how I'd pushed Cilla two days ago. Let him think I was harmless when I was outside a mosh pit. He already had enough worries. "How's Evan?" I said before I thought better of it.

He opened his mouth like a fish. He looked like he was spilling over with something, words that twisted his gut in a knot and made him look like an old man. Then he clamped his mouth shut. He stood, leaned over, and kissed me on the forehead. "I love you, Noah," he said. He patted my arm and went to get my mom.

I didn't know if he was talking to me, or if he forgot I wasn't Evan (a lot of people got us confused because we were always together), or if he just needed to say the words. It didn't matter. Because when he patted my arm, it was like the lightest brushing of wings.

My visitors trotted through the exam room mostly in ones and twos that afternoon, kind of like animals on an ark.

Mom and Cilla came first. "I told you, nimrod. I told you that you and that girl were a bad idea, and look what happened. But no, you never listen."

"That's enough, Cilla," Mom said. She had this short figure-skater hair that made her look competent. "I'll pick us up some tacos on the way home, okay, Noah?"

"Maybe not. They're all crunchy, so they might hurt to chew," Cilla said. "Maybe a pizza. With mushrooms. And maybe sautéed onions? They're soft."

I hated onions, but I didn't remind them. They wanted to do something for me, so I let them do it.

Next came Sonia and Mr. Krajicek and Mr. Krajicek's attorney.

Mr. Krajicek was the most annoying man in Portland. He was the guy with the string of appliance stores known for the most annoying commercials on late-night TV. Nod off watching *Saturday Night Live*, and you hear this *bam bam bam!* And there's Mr. Krajicek and his military flat-top, pretending to bang on the screen. "Wake up! Wake up! It's the Craig Krajicek Wake-Up Sale!"

He shook my hand when he came in, but his smile was taut. "I want you to know that I'm not like the rest of the parents in the community who think you're a useless punker. I've always liked you, son. I'm sure we can take care of this incident in a way that's win-win."

I hated that asshole. He thought he could manipulate me, but he brought his lawyer just in case. He thought he could manipulate Sonia too, which was worse. I didn't have to see him after today, but Sonia would have to deal with him for the rest of her life.

"Sonia? Don't you have something to say to Noah?" he said. Sonia was sitting in an orange plastic chair, arms crossed, swinging her shit-kicker boots. She was going to get it later when no one was looking, and she knew it. She'd already decided she didn't care.

"I'm sorry," she said, but she glared at me as she said it.

Mr. Krajicek's smile got tighter. "Do you want to try that again, young lady?"

"I'm sure we can resolve this so it's a win-win situation," I said before he could browbeat her more.

"I'm listening," he said. Behind him, his attorney sat down and opened a briefcase.

"First of all, pay my medical bills."

"Your mother tells me you have insurance . . ."

"Pay my medical bills."

Mr. Krajicek looked at his attorney, who nodded.

"Yes, yes, I think we can do that. If you'll just sign here."

"There's more," I said.

Mr. Krajicek was running out of patience. I didn't care. I had the power and he knew it. "Pay Sonia's tuition to . . . where is it you want to go again, Sonia?"

"USC."

Mr. Krajicek's smile dropped. "I don't think you're quite aware what's at stake, son. Sonia and I have talked about this. Tuition is expensive. She's always known that if she wanted to go to college, she'd have to pay her own way. Perhaps on the GI Bill. It didn't do me any harm. In fact, it built character." He flexed a bicep. Even under his shirtsleeve I could see that whatever muscle had been there had long since turned to flab.

"Uh-huh," I said. "You and I both know how well that would work with your daughter."

"All right." He sat down and steepled his hands. "How do you suggest I come up with that kind of money?"

"You have assets," I said. "Liquidate them."

Mr. Krajicek said, "You're young, so I'm willing to cut you some slack. But my accounts are more complex than you can—"

"There's the condo in Sun Valley," Sonia said. A light shadow crossed her face. Like the flapping of a wing.

"The condo? You know how much that means to your

mother and me." Mr. Krajicek's face turned red. I didn't care what brand of bully he was right then, but he was. A bully. And I didn't have any patience for bullies.

Mr. Krajicek's attorney pulled on his sleeve. "Craig? A word, if you please?"

The two of them left for the waiting room. Sonia stood up to follow, but at the last minute came over to me. "I'm sorry about what I did to your nose," she said, and she meant it. "I hope you understand, I was just trying to defend . . . No. But you and I have this history . . . No, that won't work either, will it? Even in mosh pits there's someone around to pick you up if you fall.

"You know what I'm really ashamed of? How easy it was. It took a while, and Evan was yelling, but eventually I realized what I'd done."

"That's okay. You're built to beat on stuff."

"Just not you," Sonia said. "I still hate you a little, but everyone knows you've been beaten enough already."

Huh. Kindness. I knew how much courage it took her to admit it. She would never be my girlfriend again, but she had stood up from that chair in the corner, and she had walked back to me. One more person reappearing in my life.

"We'll see you at Jojo's tomorrow, right, Sonia? We've got work to do."

"Yeah," she said. "Evan says he's got this awesome kit, and that there's a goldfish swimming around in the kettle drum."

"Creepy-looking thing. It's got these pouches on the sides of its mouth. I think Jojo feeds it LSD."

She cracked a smile. "I gotta deal with Daddy Dearest. But thanks, Noah. I'll see you tomorrow."

This time when she walked away, it was okay. This time I knew she'd be back.

Which was good, because there was more at stake than she knew.

She was a fighter.

I would need as much help as I could get to fight the Marr.

That much I remembered.

EVAN INSISTED ON STAYING OVER AT MY HOUSE that night. Usually I stayed at his place. The basement in his house was so much better. His sofa had this flower pattern and it didn't smell like fungus. Mrs. Tillstrom had the white carpet shampooed every other week. Even his basement's bathroom was better, with these fingertip towels and little soaps shaped like seashells. Then there were all the perks: the Atari, the Betamax, and the big-screen color TV.

But the night his dad stitched me up, he wanted to stay at my place. He'd only done it once before, and I was never going to forget it.

Two months after Dad's accident, Evan busted open the door to my dark room, where I lay curled around a pillow with my face to the wall, and said, "Look, I heard your mom talking to the real estate agent. Your house isn't selling. Everyone knows what happened. No one wants to buy the place."

I told him he couldn't be right, that we'd had tons of prospective buyers tromping through.

"Yeah, but I bet they spend most of their time in the basement, don't they? They're ghouls, man. Fucking ghouls." He sat down next to me. "It's time to face facts, Noah. Your mom's taking the house off the market. We have to stay put. We have to get used to it."

I turned my face from the wall and looked at him. Hard to believe he'd been there the day I tried to clean up what Dad had done. You wouldn't know it to look at him. He looked like a normal thirteen-year-old kid. He had peach fuzz growing on his cheeks that he called a beard. He'd gotten his growth spurt and was so tall and gangly it looked like he was walking on stilts.

That day, when he helped me turn away from my bedroom wall, he said, "Come on, Noah. Time to watch crappy horror movies."

He took me by the hand and led me downstairs, past the front door, and kept going down.

No. No no no. I didn't want to go downstairs, because no matter how much everyone told me that Dad was gone, that he couldn't hurt me anymore, I knew he was going to come back, and this time he would take me with him, the way he'd meant to.

Evan didn't let go of me, and before I knew it I was

running my toes through plush, orange shag carpet that hadn't been there the month before, looking at walls that had been repainted a mustardy yellow, because there was no paint white enough to bleach what Dad had done.

"See?" Evan said, taking a couple of cans of Fresca from the fridge and popping them open. "It's just a room now. You're totally safe."

I was still petrified, but Evan smiled his lopsided smile. He was working so hard at making things okay, I felt like I had to do something.

I'll just pretend *I'm all right,* I thought. *For Evan's sake.*

And I made the three steps across the carpet to take the Fresca.

I'm pretty sure that was why, on the day Sonia ripped the safety pin out of my nose, Ev wanted to spend the night in my crappy basement instead of his good one.

He had all the gewgaws. All I had was a black-and-white set with tinfoiled rabbit ears.

I suppose Evan didn't care.

He just wanted to remind me how to be strong.

So Mom pulled out the plaid sofa, which had a really thin and gritty mattress inside. Ev unrolled our sleeping bags with the hunter's plaid lining, and we settled in for a long night.

After watching me touch the packing on my face

for about the thousandth time, Ev got fed up and said, "Come on, man. Both nostrils are still there. Dad says so. But I mean, wouldn't that be cool if you'd lost your nose completely? Like, maybe if my dad tossed it into some bucket that he didn't know was radioactive and it turned into a mutant and crawled out into the night, sniffing out hot babes to terrorize?" He made a fake B-movie scream and held up his hands in terror.

I mumbled something about there not being too many hot babes left in town to wreak havoc on, and he said, "Okay, then, it'll have to terrorize Cleveland."

When I asked how my radioactive nose would get to Cleveland, he said, "All alien invaders start in Cleveland. Everyone knows that."

Except the ones that start in Portland and suck the life out of you little by little so at first you don't even notice a piece of you has disappeared.

Ev took my silence to mean I was tired, so he turned over and pulled a giant turd-shaped bottle out of his messenger bag. He thought I didn't see him taking out a huge handful of meds and swallowing them dry. When he turned back and saw me looking at him, he said, "Migraines, man. They're a bitch."

I reached over to the coffee table next to me and offered him dry Smurfberry Crunch cereal, 'cause that was good eatin'.

It was the kind of night we used to have, marathoning really bad horror movies. First we watched *The Blob*. Then *Attack of the Killer Tomatoes*, and, since I insisted, *The Man Who Fell to Earth*. Which Ev said was "weird" and fell asleep in the middle of. His right lip flapped when he snored. I kept watching the movie.

Then I'm pretty sure I fell asleep too. Or not. I was getting the two confused these days.

All I knew was that when the movie was over, Bowie's character turned to the screen and said, *It's okay to remember, Noah.*

I told him to fuck off, that I was trying to sleep, which was hard enough now that the numbing was wearing off and the stitches in my nose were itching.

You'll be okay, lad. There was no hitch in his voice. He was completely confident.

My last thought before my nose stopped itching and I sank into my sleeping bag was: Maybe he's right. Maybe this time, if I do what he says, I'll make it to the other side.

I dreamed about the *second* time my father left.

The first time, with the deer, I blamed Mom. She shouldn't have talked back to him. Dad's moods were bad, but the backlash was always worse. It would've been easier for her to clean out deer guts.

The second time he left, though, it was because of me.

I don't remember what I did to piss him off. I think I probably tracked mud on the carpet. For that, he pushed me down the stairs. Twelve stitches, grade 2 concussion, which Dr. Tillstrom said was an impressive amount of damage, even for me.

It was bad enough that when we got back from Gresham Urgent Care, Mom packed a bag for Dad and kicked him out. Dad cried and said he was sorry and he could change, but she didn't give. When he saw the pathetic drunk act wasn't going to work on her, he called her a bitch and told her that he paid the bills, goddamn it, and he had every right to stay.

Cilla and I were in my room at the time, Cilla running her hands through my hair and humming "Space Oddity." Mom had stationed her there to wake me up every half hour 'cause of the concussion. I woke up every so often to hear her sing about floating above the world.

She sang off-key and the words were lovely, but it wasn't enough to drown out what was going on outside my bedroom.

The two of us heard every word of Mom and Dad's fight. Especially when Mom threatened to call the police and show them what he'd done to my head.

Then the front door slammed and Mom ran through the house, locking everything, getting ready for a siege that wasn't long in coming.

When Cilla and I woke up the next morning, Mom was in the kitchen, looking fifty years older than she had the night before. She was red-eyed and jittery, eating Folgers Crystals straight out of the can. She shook them into her mouth and got little flakes all over her lipstick. "I've gotta go to the office. Do you want me to drop you at the bus stop?" It was 6:15. The bus didn't come until 7:30.

When we didn't answer, Mom looked at her watch and swore. "Goddamn. I don't have time for this. Why can't schools be more accommodating to single mothers?" She pointed a chipped nail at us. "Stay here until the last minute, do you understand? Don't open the door for anyone. When you leave, leave together. If your dad shows up, keep him at a distance. Whatever you do, don't let him touch you. Got it?"

I didn't understand why we needed that particular warning. Of course we wouldn't let him touch us.

"It's okay, Mom. We'll be fine," Cilla said, and hummed as though everything was hunky-dory.

Mom kissed both of us on the forehead, took her briefcase, and walked off, mumbling, "Locksmith, attorney . . . Cilla! Lock the door behind me! I mean it. Use the dead bolt."

Cilla followed her downstairs and did what she asked, then came back up to the living room. I leaned over the back of the sofa and watched Mom, briefcase in hand, taking out her car keys.

And then he was there. He caught her wrist and swung her around, pinning her to the driver's door. I still don't know where he came from.

Cilla caught her breath. "Check the dead bolt, Noah," she said.

"What about Mom? She's alone out there."

"We have to trust her," Cilla said. "She's going to have to handle him eventually. If it gets bad we'll call Idiot Willy. You know their phone number, right?"

I did. Crock and I had been riding bikes, skateboarding, and playing with our garden hoses since we were two years old. His phone number was stitched into my skull.

I made a move for the phone. "Not yet," Cilla said, putting a hand on my arm. "Wait."

We couldn't hear much of what Dad said since the window was closed. I heard *please*. I heard *I'm sorry*. I heard *baby*. But his eyes said *I'm not done with you yet. If you take me in now, you'll pay. If you wait to take me back, you'll pay even more.*

Dad deserved a fucking Oscar for the performance he put on that morning. It was all for the neighbors. He was trying to look like the victim, and he was beginning to pull it off. Around the cul-de-sac, window curtains pulled back. Housewives in foamy pink curlers rubbed their eyes and stared at my mother as if to say, *Let him in already so we can get back to sleep.*

Cilla stood looking out the window, still wearing her football jersey nightshirt, a box of Froot Loops held loosely at her side.

"You don't think she'll fall for it this time, do you?" I said.

"Hope not," Cilla said, which wasn't nearly reassuring

enough. Then she started humming again, which is how I knew we were in trouble.

The scene in the driveway seemed to go on forever, Mom cornered, Dad trying to appear the wronged spouse.

The box of cereal in Cilla's hand started to shake, even though if you looked at Cilla's face she seemed frozen as a statue. My sister was terrified. If Mom let Dad in the door, we had no chance. After he was done bashing us, we'd spend the rest of our lives bringing him beer and tacos from Taco Bell when he demanded them (nine tacos, three for a dollar, seven for him, two for us). Who knows? We might wind up stuffing his next kill.

We might *be* his next kill.

Now Mom leaned on the rear door of her car, trying to hide the fact that she was crying, which I didn't understand. Crying was a good thing. It might work in her favor in the cul-de-sac of public opinion.

Cilla shook her head. "I don't like the way this is going. We're in for a real shitstorm," she said. "Get your clothes on. When it looks like he's coming in, go out the back door. Run to Evan's. Stay there until I call you."

I ran down the hall and put on a pair of grungy jeans, a T-shirt, and my Members Only jacket. I was ready to run. When I came back into the living room, Cilla was standing where I had left her, looking out the front window, humming louder than ever.

And seeing her there, in her raggedy nightshirt, her

hair ratted, I realized: She may act like a know-it-all, but she's just a kid like me.

Most kids can't point to an exact moment when they grow up, but I can, and that was it.

Run out the back, Cilla said. What a cowardly thing to do. All my life I'd let them try to protect me. Why should I be the one who escaped? Why couldn't Mom and Cilla escape too? For as long as I could remember, they'd done their best to protect me from Dad.

I knew what I had to do.

It was my turn.

I went down to the basement to the stuffed head of the red-tailed deer that was hanging above the bar. It was Dad's first kill, and Mom complained about it not because it was gross but because he'd paid the taxidermist with money she'd saved for Cilla's braces.

It was a disgusting thing, that deer head, with marble eyes and mangy neck fur. It always gave me the creeps because the expensive taxidermist couldn't even make it look half alive.

I ripped that red-tailed deer off the wall, went upstairs to the living room, and threw open the window.

Cilla's eyes popped, seeing me struggle with the stupid head.

"Make sure we're locked down," I said.

She went to check on the back door, and reinforced the sliding glass with a dowel. We were barricaded inside.

I called down to Mom, "Get in the car. Leave now."

Dad released her to look up at me. That was all she needed in order to weasel away from his grip and into the Datsun, slamming the door behind her. She backed up without looking and peeled out like an Indy 500 driver.

When she was gone, I pitched that mangy trophy out the window, hoping the antlers would catch Dad in the eye. They didn't. The head landed in the hydrangeas underneath the window.

"What do you think you're doing, Noah?" Dad called, not even trying to sound reasonable now.

I ignored him, because I wasn't done. If Mom wasn't strong enough to get this asshole out of our lives, I had to be.

I went into their bedroom and threw his Dickies coveralls and flannel shirts out the window, one by one. Then I went to the laundry basket and upended the whole thing on his head. It gave me a warm fuzzy feeling to see that some of his BVD undies had skid marks on them and all the neighbors could see them.

In the basement I found and threw out:

1. A twenty-four-pack of PfefferBrau Porter;
2. A calendar that came from some auto insurance company that showed topless girls on Harleys;
3. All his crappy seventies albums, like the Nitty Gritty Dirt Band, Don McLean, and Emerson, Lake & Palmer.

It gave me great pleasure to wing all these out the window, Frisbee style. The Santana album brained him, somersaulted, then rolled to a halt in the street behind him. He picked it up from the middle of the road and pulled the record out of the sleeve, only to have it shatter into a million pieces of vinyl around his feet.

Cilla was beside me again. "I hope that wasn't what I think it was," she said, but she was smiling.

I smirked. "Hell yeah."

Without taking her eyes off my father, she said to me, "God, you're stupid, nimrod," as she ruffled my hair.

Dad lunged for the front door.

Cilla and I took a step backward, away from the window. "Everything locked?" I said.

Cilla nodded. "Locked. Doweled. Latched. Deadbolted. Won't keep him from shooting out a window, though."

Dad's gun rack with the guns was on the back of his pickup. I had no idea where that was, but he had to have gotten here somehow.

Cilla and I hugged each other and cowered in a corner while Dad pounded on the door. "Open this door, you goddamn freaks!"

Then the pounding stopped.

Cilla and I got up from our crouch and dared to look.

Across the street, Idiot Willy had come out on his front porch wearing a ratty old terry cloth robe that barely covered his old-school law enforcement officer doughnut gut. He was sitting on the woven-plastic porch swing, surrounded by a dozen red, white, and blue birdhouses. I don't know why Crock's mom liked them, since none of those things ever held any actual birds.

Willy had a shotgun on his lap and he was quietly cleaning it. He sat there, and as the swing creaked back and forth, he cleaned his gun, sanding it to nothing, sighting things through the view finder, looking for all the world like that was what people normally did at 6:45 in the morning on their front porch.

Even though everything about the setup over there was tacky—the birdhouses, the cheap porch swing, Idiot Willy's ratty old robe—I'd never been so impressed with anyone in my whole life.

Dad stared up at me through the window, knowing his show had failed. No one believed he was Mr. Wronged Husband and Father.

To this day I don't know which of us should get credit for the save—Idiot Willy or me.

But I know who Dad blamed.

He stood in the driveway below us, surrounded by his dirty underwear, his cheap beer, his stuffed red-tailed deer that no longer had a tail.

"You little *punk*," he said. I should have been afraid, but I wasn't. It was the best compliment I'd ever gotten in my life. He didn't know that punk was a new kind of music. He just thought I was an asshole.

So I did exactly what I shouldn't have done.

I laughed. I may have pointed too, at him and his dirty underwear and the Harley calendar. Now everyone knew what he was about.

Dad gathered up his stuff the best he could and skulked off to wherever he'd left his truck. He left shards and rags of his life on the front lawn.

"You shouldn't have done that, Noah," Cilla said when he was gone. "He'll find a way to get back at us. But you know what? I'm glad you did." She ruffled my hair, then trotted off to her room, humming "Heroes" by David Bowie.

I'd done it. For the first time in my life, I'd stood up to my father.

I closed my eyes and savored the moment—because I knew it wouldn't last.

Cilla was right. Dad would feel like I'd cheated him out of something.

He'd be back.

THE DAY AFTER SONIA SCARRED MY NOSE, when Crock, Ev, and I were eating our soggy tuna sandwiches in the school cafeteria, Sonia and Jaime came trotting up to us.

Sonia banged her tray on the table so hard everyone's food jumped.

"That was awesome!" she said. Then, in her dad's cheesy TV commercial voice, said, "'Do you know how much that little punk cost me? We had to sell our condo in Sun Valley to pay your tuition. Stay away from him.' I'm thinking about telling him we're engaged. So, what does Jojo call that place where we're rehearsing? We have to cut the demo in a couple of weeks, right?"

"The Maxi Pad," Evan said, picking onions out of his sandwich.

Sonia's smile got bigger. "Sounds disgusting. I can't

wait to tell my father. Hey, are you gonna eat that?" She pointed at the pickle on Ev's plate.

"No," he said, pushing the entire tray across the table. "Here. Take the whole thing. I'm not hungry."

Evan was rarely hungry these days. Usually he didn't eat at all on the days his skin was red, which was about once a month.

He had some name for it. Derma-blah-blah-blah.

I still didn't understand why a rash would affect his appetite.

Sonia just about had a seizure when she uncovered Jojo's drums. "Oh my god! Are these Ludwig Vistalites? Hi-hat! Floor tom! Snare drum! Crash cymbal! Rototom! Bongos! *Goldfish!*"

Sure enough, the floor tom was filled with water and there was a goldfish swimming around in it.

"That's Castaneda. He's on a higher plane of existence. Here ya go, fella." Jojo lifted the lid and sprinkled something in the water that could've been fish flakes or could have been weed.

The bottom of the snare was lined with really round rocks, some of which had strings attached to them.

"Jojo," I said, "what's that floating on the bottom of the snare? You know, underneath Castaneda?"

"Probably cherry bombs."

"Defused, right?" I said.

Jojo thought real hard. "Hey, anyone want a doobie?"

All through this exchange, Ziggy sat on the window-sill, flicking cigarette ash into the muggy air. "Right," he said, flicking the butt out to the street. "Let's get to work, shall we?"

That first week we mostly rehearsed the campy pieces I'd written: "Pong Warrior," "All the Best Aliens Land in Cleveland," and "Volkswagen Madonna."

Jaime thought it was hilarious. Sonia had to explain it to Crock, who hadn't been there when I busted my nose.

"The song's about *Jaime*? Running red lights in nothing but a bra and miniskirt?" Crock said. Apparently his skank sonar was intact. Honestly? I'd forgotten he was even there. He came and went a lot. Filling out paper-work for us, trolling the Acropolis Tavern for watery beer and trashy women, and helping Jojo in the store.

Now he was practically slobbering on Jojo's alpaca carpet. Over Jaime. I didn't like it one bit, but before I could say anything, Evan did.

"Shut up, Crock. And stop staring at Jaime's tits. Can we get back to work, please?"

Thank god for Ziggy. He was always there when we opened the frosted glass door of the Maxi Pad, always in the same spot: staring out the window, smoking, cool in a thousand-dollar suit.

He knew exactly what my songs needed and wasn't shy about telling me. He would pull me out onto the landing and say, "Those songs are fine for a warm-up, lad. But it's not going to be good enough to get rid of the Marr at its source."

I would tell him thank you.

He would grab my shoulders and say, "I know you understand the severity of the situation. You're up against an evil that can't be taken on directly. If you don't give this everything you have, more girls will disappear. *Evan* will disappear completely."

Once or twice I tried to pin him down: What exactly was the Marr, other than a black cloud that consumes everything in its path, and has decided to settle here?

"Best think of it as a curse, son. It feeds on living tissue. No regard for how healthy or old you are. It picks its victims at random. Jurgen has found a way to feed off it, god knows how. We have to stop him. In order to do that, we have to get into the PfefferBrau Haus."

Most days I flipped him off, but he didn't seem to care.

"Never mind, Noah," he reassured me. "Just keep practicing. It'll come."

He was right. My breakthrough came on a Saturday night. Our demo was due at the PfefferBrau Haus that Monday.

We had just put the finishing touches on "6:00 Curfew," about Evan's mom always calling the Maxi Pad and wanting him home to rest. (Jojo really liked that song, probably because we thrashed so hard we practically shredded his instruments into matchsticks. "Whoa. You guys are gonna rock the joint. Speaking of joints, anyone seen my doobie?"

"In the kitchen cabinet. By the spice rack," Jaime said.)

We all felt good, and we wanted to be rested for the next day, when we cut our tape. Everyone was already packing up their gear and cleaning kung pao chicken from Jojo's plates, when Ziggy whispered, "Now's the time, lad, if you've got it."

I still had my guitar out and was strumming random chords.

Okay, then, I thought. *Here goes.*

I took a deep breath. "Wait," I told everyone. "I've got something else I've been working on. I want you to hear it."

There was lots of groaning. Jaime slammed the silverware she'd been cleaning in the sink with a giant clatter. "Come on, Noah," she said. "We're tired. We're good enough. Even Jojo says so."

"I know what I'm asking. Please. Give it just one listen. It won't take long. And if you don't like it, we'll save it for later."

I looked at Evan's face. It was one of his starved, sunburned days. I didn't need Ziggy to tell me that he was running out of later. We only had now.

Before I could change my mind, I played the opening progression of "Disappearing."

Your picture's everywhere
The ink fades, images fall
I still see your outline
As you melt into a wall

I see your pain
Tacked to the board so long
Colors fade
But yours are strong

I stopped. I didn't realize I'd closed my eyes until I opened them and Jojo was standing over me. Before I knew it, he wrapped me a bear hug. Which would have been really nice if it weren't for the pot smell. It was kind of like being hugged by a frizzy-haired, middle-aged bong.

He stood back. It looked like he was crying. But then again, he could've just been stoned. "All those girls," he said, shaking his head. "All those families not knowing . . . that's an awesome tribute, Noah. You guys better get it right."

"Tribute? *Tribute?* Aren't you forgetting that people are still hoping to get their girls back *alive?*" Jaime said. "That song isn't a tribute. It's a funeral march."

Evan unstrapped his bass and stalked off into the stairwell, slamming the door behind him.

He knew the song wasn't about any girl.

I ran after him and nearly tripped over his scrawny carcass seated on the top step. He was bent double and running his fingers through his dreads.

"Don't, Noah," he said without looking up.

"Don't what?"

"Say or do anything. Just don't."

I stood over him in silence for a few minutes. He wanted me to leave him alone, but I couldn't. He was here. And as long as he was, I would be too.

"Jaime didn't know what she was saying," I finally said. "She thought I was talking about total strangers. They all did. Nobody knows you're sick."

It wasn't exactly a lie. Jaime kind of knew, and the others may have guessed.

Evan said nothing. He hugged himself as if he would fall apart.

"It was a bad idea. Let's just forget it and go home," I said.

He whipped around and glared at me. "Who says I want to forget it? It's a good song, Noah. I'll be back in. Just gimme a sec to get out from under this black cloud."

I backed away, knowing that it wasn't any regular black cloud he was dealing with. This one was chewing at him piece by piece.

• • •

Ev was as good as his word, and we stayed through the night, putting the finishing touches on "Disappearing."

The sun was coming up, and our demo was cut by the time we dribbled out of Jojo's in the morning.

To get to my car, we walked past the Fish Grotto, and the same homeless guy with the tinfoil hat was slouching against a wall. Jojo knew him. Said his name was Terrence. And he slipped Terrence singles whenever he walked past.

That day, Terrence wasn't asleep, but he wasn't really awake either. He stared at nothing and muttered something that sounded like "Blah blah blah should've seen blah blah blah."

The dude needed a shower and a nap. I knew what that felt like, so I tucked a five-dollar bill in his jacket pocket.

On the drive home, Ev pretended to be asleep, leaning against the window. The color was slowly draining from his skin.

He must've gotten tired of me checking on him at every stop light, so halfway home, he stirred himself and said, "Please. I promise I'll tell you, Noah. Just not right now, okay? I'm really tired."

"All right," I said, thinking that was the end of it.

It wasn't. He closed his eyes and spoke again. His voice was softer and smoother than Ziggy's could ever be. It was like he was whispering to me from across the universe.

"Let's just say what I've got can't be cured by Smurf-berry Crunch cereal."

And even though I already knew it, I felt my veins thrill with frozen bile.

Sssoooon, I heard the Marr hiss. *Sssoooon.*

THAT NIGHT I DIDN'T NEED ZIGGY to command me to dream.

It was about my dad again. All the images spewing from my brain at night were about my dad.

It was the same day I threw all of Dad's crap out on the front lawn. I made it to school in one piece, then trembled my way through seven periods of seventh grade. Teachers pounced on me for not paying attention. But how could I? Dad said he'd be back, and he never made empty threats. Some kids say their parents are gonna kill them for something they've done, but they didn't mean it the way I did.

Dad had a shotgun. He was pissed at me. He said he'd be back.

• • •

When I came home, Dad's stuff I'd tossed out was still on the front lawn. His shirts had drifted into the neighbors' yard, but otherwise our grass was a trash heap.

Dad's truck still wasn't in the driveway, so I thought either he'd hid it or he wasn't there.

I tested the front door. Still locked, thank god. I took out my key and opened the door. Then I stood on the landing for a second and listened. Not a sound.

I don't know how long I stood on the entrance landing, between the upstairs and the downstairs, trying to decide what to do next.

Slowly, I started to relax. I went to the kitchen and fixed myself a peanut butter and jelly sandwich. I discovered we were low on milk, so I went downstairs to get more from the fridge in the basement.

And that's where I found him, sitting calmly on the piano bench, his hunting rifle pointed at, but not already in, his mouth.

He was red-faced and crying without making a sound. If I hadn't been so afraid I would've been ashamed. He was a lump of a man sitting there. The gun looked so much bigger than him.

But I *was* afraid. He was here. He had a gun. He was not acting. I didn't know what desperation was then, but I recognized its face.

"You think you can get rid of me that easily, you little punk? Shame me in front of the whole neighborhood?

Well, let me tell you something. They all know what you're about. And if they don't, they soon will."

And he pulled the trigger.

It's crazy what you think about in times like that. Even as I cleaned pieces of his head off the walls, I thought: *Shit, this'll never come out. Dad's gonna kill me.* I didn't think even once that it was over, that Dad was on the floor without a jaw or a brain, because I'd covered it with a towel.

I'd forgotten that Evan was coming by later so we could shoot hoops. I'd forgotten I'd left the front door unlocked. So I only knew he was there when I heard him say, "My god, Noah. What have you done?"

I turned around. I was wearing rubber gloves and holding a bloody sponge. There was a bucket of water at my feet that was bright pink.

And there was what was left of Dad.

To this day I don't know what Evan saw in my face. I don't know if he changed his mind about my guilt, or if he didn't care. He disappeared into the garage and came back with the other giant sponge and a bucket of bleach. "You're using dishwashing liquid," he said. "It'll never come out."

And he started helping me clean.

After about an hour, he said, "I think that's the best we can do. I'd better get Idiot Willy before your mom and sister come home. They're not gonna want to see this."

The rest comes to me in pieces. I'm sitting on the front stoop. There are police cars and ambulances all around, and someone's thrown a blanket over me. But since Ev won't leave me, they have to throw a blanket over both of us. Someone hands us foam cups of coffee, which taste foul but at least are warm.

I remember Idiot Willy talking to me. I remember thinking that I'd never seen him up close, and that his gut was even bigger than I thought, and he had craters for pores.

He flipped open a tiny notebook and said, "Your mom's on her way. I know you didn't do this, Noah. We found a note. He blamed everybody but himself." He shook his head. "Son of a bitch. I wish he were still alive so I could shoot him at close range. Honestly, what kind of asshole does this to his own son?"

I stared across the street to the collection of birdhouses on Willy's porch. They seemed so *normal*.

"I need to know why you cleaned up," Idiot Willy went on. "I think I understand, but they're asking."

He jutted his chin toward the guys in uniforms coming in and out of the house. There were lots of them.

To me the answer was obvious. "He always hated a mess."

Idiot Willy didn't look at me like I was crazy, even though my answer was totally batshit.

"That's what I thought." He flipped his notebook closed. Even his sigh was heavy. "At least now you're free."

I didn't feel free. I wouldn't feel free ever again.

But at least there was the warmth of the coffee. And Evan's scrawny shoulder against mine as we sat under scratchy orange blankets. Both of us were scrawny. Together, we almost made one whole kid.

15

THE WEEK AFTER WE CUT OUR DEMO, we wandered around the city blank-eyed and confused, like we'd woken up in some alien landscape. A really swampy one. The air around us was thick and stinky with hops, and even though it was spring, it didn't rain, so there was nothing to wash away the boredom.

Crock told us it was too soon for him to make *Whaddya think?* runs to the PfefferBrau Haus to see if we made the cut, but we went to Jojo's every afternoon anyway. We jammed in the Maxi Pad and helped mind the store. Everyone got their homework done on time. Sonia helped us with our French (*"Voilà la tour Eiffel"*), and Crock wrote our personal finance papers for us. Five of them. All different, each culled from the *Wall Street Journal.* "Hey, I can spot a trend," he said.

I worried he was turning into a Republican, even

though he still said President Reagan was a walking corpse.

We threw open all the windows in the Maxi Pad, hoping the cross breeze would help with the stagnant air, but all it did was cycle the brewery smell through faster. The windows didn't open in the store below, so it smelled like mold. Watermarks above Country Western oozed yellow goo that looked like pus.

Looking at that swollen ceiling, I couldn't help thinking it was only a matter of time until something crashed down on all our heads. And I was right.

It just wasn't what we'd expected.

We were walking to Jojo's on Friday afternoon. Ev offered us chocolate-covered espresso beans. Sonia was his only taker, and she didn't need them since she was naturally espressoed. She decided it would be a really good idea to walk over the tops of parked cars instead of with us on the sidewalk. She didn't break anything, but she left bootprints on people's windshields and hoods. Thank god she didn't try it with Ginny.

As we walked, I couldn't help constantly touching my nose, like she was trouncing it all over again. The packing had come off, but the stitches were still there, and they itched like crazy. Crock said keeping them lubricated was the answer, but the way he said it made antibiotic ointment sound X-rated.

We were chatting about things that were not the

PfefferFest. I don't remember what. Something some idiot jock in school had said, how Scott Freeland's mom and dad were getting divorced so Scott had started sneaking Jägermeister into his locker.

I didn't realize right away that we'd left Evan behind, and when I did, needles of terror spiked through me. Oh, crap. He'd looked fine when he'd gotten out of the car. Was he curled on the pavement with another bone-crushing headache?

No. He was just standing a block back, staring into the distance like a zombie. "Something's happening," he said in a way that made me think the Marr was making a final push and we weren't ready for it.

I craned my neck to see what Ev was looking at. There was a small crowd in front of the Fish Grotto. Maybe a dozen people, watching something we couldn't see that made a noise like an air-raid siren. A siren that swore. A lot.

"Goddamn you! I'll fuckyourshitup!"

I didn't think it was the Marr, because I didn't feel cold. This was something else.

We inched closer. I knew him by smell before I knew him by sight. Because, honestly? Without the foil hat, Terrence looked like this man-sized heap of poop.

That heap was being "sirred" by two of Portland's Finest. "Sir, I'm going to have to ask you to come with us now, sir."

"Isn't that Terrence?" Crock said.

This wasn't right. I didn't know what was going on, but we passed Terrence every day. We'd gotten used to him. We gave him money when we had it, and he smiled a harmless smile when he took it. He wouldn't accept money from the girls no matter how sneaky they tried to be, tucking it in his pocket when he was asleep. He always found out and brought the money back to Jojo's, slamming it on the counter. "I don't prey on little girls. Not like that sick fuck in the suit." And he'd spit a gob of green phlegm on the floor for us to mop up.

As we came closer, Terrence morphed from a swearing pile of poop to a swearing mound of dirty beige clothes with a pasty white knob on top.

He was almost completely bald. The skin on his shiny dome was pale, uncorrupted by grime or sun damage. He had a fringe of greasy white hair above his ears, but that didn't hide the hole in his skull.

Wait, what? I looked again to be sure. And there it was—a hole. It wasn't bleeding or anything; it was just a circle an inch around where there was no bone, just a dent of scar tissue covering something blue and throbbing. Artery? Brain?

I really didn't want to know if it was brain. Brains were only okay when they were cheesy effects in black-and-white movies. You know, the kind that crawled out of jars and chased helpless secretaries—not the kind you could see through scar tissue, or the kind you had to bleach off walls.

"No wonder he keeps it covered," Crock said. "That's nasty."

Evan's hands went to his dreads, and any color left in his face drained out of it. "Do you think he's had surgery?" he said.

I didn't think it looked neat enough to be surgical, but I didn't say so. This wasn't the time for us to bystand. I hadn't had to do that kind of cleanup in years, and I wasn't eager to do it now.

The two policemen, in tinted aviator glasses, were trying to get him to move. One of them, the blond, didn't look much older than us, and he was twitchy. The other guy, the Filipino, was short, but so thick around the pecs that he looked like Arnold Schwarzenegger.

They both had their gun holsters unsnapped.

The Filipino tried to keep his voice even. "Sir, we're going to need you to come with us. Sir, please, if you'll come this way . . ."

Terrence was crying, telling them no. "I have to keep watch," he said. "I already let one gal slip away. If you lock me up, another one'll disappear."

I felt like I'd just crunched down on a chocolate espresso bean. My brain was suddenly racing.

I wormed my way through the gawkers. "Who?" I said. "Who'll disappear?"

Ev tried to pull me back. "Stay out of it, Noah."

I wrenched myself away from Evan, just like Terrence wrenched himself away from the guys with the handcuffs.

"Who'll disappear?" I asked again.

I looked into his face. Crying had carved rivers in the grime on his cheeks. The whites of his eyes were yellow, like someone had peed in them. "I sawr him. I sawr him go out. He's wearing his suit. On the hunt again. I tried to tell them but they won't listen. Gotta help the gals."

Oh my god. The freak in the suit. He was talking about Jurgen Pfeffer. I'd been sure he'd wait until the Pfeffer-Fest to kill again. All this work I'd done to get access to the PfefferBrau Haus, and it never occurred to me that Jurgen and whatever he was brewing couldn't wait that long.

I looked back at Evan, the only other one who knew how I felt about the Disappearing Girls. But he was no help. He was leaning on the hood of a Datsun 280ZX like it was the only thing keeping him semi-vertical. He shook pain pills out of his giant turd-shaped bottle.

I'd have to worry about him later. Right now there was a situation.

Crock strode forward with his confident businessman's swagger. "Excuse me, officers. What's going on here?"

Crock got "sirred" too. The Filipino put a hand up in a stop gesture. "Step away, sir."

"Hey, it's okay. You probably know my stepdad. Willy MacInnes?"

Then a bunch of things happened at once. The baby cop made another grab for Terrence, and this time when Terrence jerked away, he reached into his pocket and pulled out something dull and metallic. He swung it in a broad arc through the thick air in front of him.

The officers pulled their guns from their holsters and trained them on him. The whole thing was so quick it looked staged. Knife, guns. Point, counterpoint. Don't miss your cue 'cause it'll be quick.

But this wasn't an act. Someone was going to get hurt.

"Whoa whoa whoa!" Crock said, putting his hands in the air and backing away toward Evan and the girls behind the 280ZX. Random gawkers found something else to do real quick. In an instant, Terrence had changed this from a spectacle to a war zone.

"Noah." I heard Evan's voice as if it were underwater. "Get back."

Get back to what? Couldn't he see I was trying to figure out a pattern here? Because there was one. I knew it.

"Sir. Put the knife down. Sir, you don't wanna do this. Sir . . ."

Terrence didn't put it down. He didn't lunge either. He didn't want to hurt anyone. He only wanted to be heard.

"You don't understand. Nobody understands. He's left. He never leaves unless he's found a victim."

"Who's left, Terrence? Who is it?" I said. "Tell me!" I would've grabbed him and shaken the answer out of him if I could, but his blade was still up.

Even I wasn't that stupid.

I remember seeing something yellow just behind my right shoulder, and the next thing I knew, Ziggy was standing with us.

Looking at him, I understood what made the real Bowie such a star. 'Cause when Ziggy showed up, there was no doubt who was in command. It wasn't the guys with the badges and guns, it wasn't the crazy homeless guy with the knife, and it certainly wasn't a bunch of teenage punks.

He walked between the police and Terrence, nodding discreetly at all of them. Then he kept walking. He saw what the rest of us had missed: Terrence's tinfoil crown, which had rolled down the street and come to rest next to Anteek Comix.

He picked it up, dusted it off on the sleeve of his silk shirt, strode calmly between the police and the homeless guy, and replaced the crown on Terrence's head.

He put a smooth hand on Terrence's shoulder and, in a voice that would have quieted a raging tiger, said, "Give me the knife, old son. I'll keep it safe until you get out."

Terrence's hand shook, but it was all right. Soon enough, the blade arm went flaccid.

Terrence tossed the blade to his opposite hand so he could give it to Ziggy handle first, the way my dad always taught me.

When it was in the air, the policemen fired.

Bang! I felt the recoil in my eardrums. I shut my eyes

and squatted into a crouch. For a second I thought the sidewalk itself was spinning.

When the reverb from the gun stopped pounding my head, I popped an eye open. Was I hurt? No pain except in my eardrums.

But here was the big thing: Ziggy was gone. Not only gone, but I was standing in his place in front of Terrence, between him and the police. How had I gotten there? I hadn't moved my feet. Something must've pushed me. But what the hell happened to Ziggy?

I'd have to worry about that later.

I looked at the 280ZX where I'd last seen Ev. "Everyone okay?" I said. Ev waved but kept the girls down.

Crock jumped up from his crouch and rounded on the policemen. "Assholes! What the hell are you doing firing at a guy on a crowded city street? You could've hurt my friend!"

I had enough time to think, *But they didn't, so everyone's okay,* before Terrence crumpled.

He sank to his knees, yellow eyes glazing over.

The blond officer who'd fired looked stunned stupid. "I just shot a man," he said.

My hands balled to fists at my sides. If I hadn't had years of experience getting beaten around, I would've smacked the guy. Portland's Finest, shooting that poor, damaged old coot.

"Call an ambulance!" I barked at the other cop. "Crock. Jojo's got a first aid kit. Go get it. Now!"

He ran.

Before Terrence pitched forward, I caught his head and lowered him onto his back. I couldn't see any blood, so maybe he wasn't hit. I started stripping off layers of his grimy clothes, which was when I discovered the poppy blooming on his chest near his left shoulder. I pressed my hands over it. "Good news, Terrence, you're gonna be okay," I told him. All the while thinking, *Oh, crap, this is bad this is bad this is bad.* I looked up at all the people gathered around. "Anyone remember what side the heart is on?"

Something crackled on the walkie-talkies the police were wearing on their shoulders.

"You saw him," the blond police kid said. "He was throwing a knife." He'd started to come alive. And his first thought was about his own ass.

"It looked more like he was handing it over," Evan said.

"Hey, Terrence, how ya doin'?" I could tell how he was doing, and it was not good. The blood kept coming out of him.

Jaime crouched opposite me. She was breathless, like she'd been aerobicizing. "Do we sterilize it?" she said.

"With what?"

She rifled through Terrence's grimy coat, drew out a flask, and rattled it. "Still half full."

I looked at the blood welling up through my hands. Was it a good idea or not? I wished Ziggy were still here to tell me what to do. But he wasn't, so I had to muddle through. "Okay. On three. Ready?" I counted, she poured.

That had to hurt, but Terrence didn't buck or moan. He didn't do anything. The booze helped clear away the blood, so I got a good look at the hole in his chest. It looked higher than where the heart should be, but what did I know? I hadn't done CPR since . . . I'd never done CPR. All I knew was that the hole kept gushing. Oh, how it gushed.

Where the hell was Ziggy when I really needed him? That *shit*. I was gonna kick his high-thread-count ass the next time I saw him.

Sonia joined us. "I've got the kit." She showed us a plastic red briefcase.

"Great. Pull out the biggest bandages you can find and put pressure here where my hands are." I didn't hear anything being opened or ripped. Sonia wasn't moving. "What's the holdup?"

"He's so dirty," Sonia said. "Aren't you worried about diseases?"

"Give me that," Jaime said, and snatched away the red suitcase.

Jojo appeared and cradled Terrence's head on his lap. "Come on, man. You survived months in a tiger cage. You can make it through this."

"I got the bandage, Noah. Are you ready?" Jaime

said. I nodded and lifted up my hands, and she pressed gauze right into the hole. She kept her hands over the thin gauze and I covered them with mine. It didn't help. Our hands were covered in red in no time. It was like one really twisted valentine.

I had no idea how long we were hunched over him, trying to keep him together with four red hands. Then someone in a uniform was pulling me away. I jabbed an elbow at him and screamed, "Let me go! Haven't you already done enough?"

"Hey hey hey! Easy, man," Jojo said, right up in my face. "It's not the pigs. Different uniform. See the gloves? These guys are here to help."

He was right. I looked around. The whole street was lit up like a dance club, red lights flashing in the sky. The guy I'd elbowed had short white sleeves. There were at least five others like him, carrying big kits and barking at each other. One of them slapped an oxygen mask over Terrence's face. They were working fast, which I figured was a good thing. If they were working slowly or not at all, *that* would've been bad.

"Come on, man," Jojo said, urging me away. "Let's go inside. You don't need to see this."

"But I want to," I said. I had to know what it was like to save someone. I needed the practice for what was coming.

I searched the crowd for Evan's face.

He was behind the red flashing lights, leaning on Jaime, who looked like she was wearing dripping red opera gloves. Oh god, poor Jaime.

And yet she seemed to be holding up really well. With all the red around her, the lights, the blood, she seemed solid. There was no one better to have Evan leaning on. And Evan definitely needed leaning. His skin was so white it looked see-through. I felt as though I could see all of him, inside and out. He was fading away. *Please stay with me*, I thought. *You're Evan. You can't leave.*

"Get everyone inside," I told Jojo. "I'm afraid Ev's going to blow away."

"Good thinking, man," Jojo said. "He don't look too good. How long's his aura been all wonky?"

Behind me, the medics strapped Terrence on a gurney and were hustling him toward the back end of an ambulance. "Wait! He's calling for the kid!" one of them said. He motioned me closer. "Make it fast. We've gotta leave now."

I leaned over Terrence. His eyes were open. His oxygen mask was fogging up, so at least he was breathing.

He tried to take my hand but was having a hard time because he was sapped. So I took him by the forearm. It was like gripping a really weak guppy.

He motioned me closer. "You'll tell 'em?" he rasped through his mask. "Everyone's disappearing."

I nodded and squeezed his filthy palm. "I'll tell 'em," I said.

"You're a good boy." And he pressed something on me, something I hid in the sleeve of my leather jacket.

It was his knife.

THERE WAS A GRIM PARTY at the Maxi Pad that night. Sonia was squirrelly for not wanting to touch Terrence when he needed help. She tried to make up for it by splurging on a Chinese banquet, but nobody wanted her Guilt Moo Shu Pork. Ev had some on his plate but he wasn't eating it. He was just pushing bits of cabbage around with a pair of chopsticks.

Jojo gave Jaime and me T-shirts, since the ones we had were ruined. He draped Jaime in David Bowie, of course. It was the image from the *Let's Dance* album cover, the one where Bowie wears boxing gloves and there are dance steps floating in the air above him.

Since I had my pick, I wanted a Clash T-shirt, but Sonia picked out a different one for me. It had a blue-and-red bull's-eye in the middle, the kind favored by

British drummers. Ev had a problem with it, though. He thought I was sending the wrong message.

"Goddamn, Noah, you're not a target," he said when Sonia held it up to me. He pushed his plate of uneaten food away. "You put yourself in the middle of a standoff. With guns, you shithead. Why the hell didn't you come away when I told you? What if it'd been you with the sucking chest wound? Did you ever stop to think how I'd feel?"

"I didn't get between the cops and Terrence. Ziggy did. He's the one who found the tinfoil hat."

Ev threw up his hands. "I don't feel like playing right now, Noah."

Playing? Did he say I'd been *playing*? What the hell was up his butt? Never mind. He'd been popping pills all afternoon. Let him have his I'm-not-eating-or-making-polite-conversation funk. He'd get over it.

I took my bull's-eye T-shirt and ducked into the bathroom to change. One of the girls had put a wicker basket of potpourri on the toilet tank, so the room smelled like cinnamon dried in vinegar—spicy and tart at the same time. Above the sink hung a mirror that was more ancient than Jojo, with curlicues of frosted glass around the borders, and flecks all over where the reflective surface had worn off. Looking at my face in it, I felt like little bits of me were flaking off too.

I was taking off my jacket, to wash my hands and

change my shirt, when Terrence's knife fell out. I'd actually forgotten about it for five minutes.

Now I picked it up and took a good look.

It was eight inches long, with a four-inch drop point. Rubber handle.

I held it up to the light.

It was rusted over and sticky, but I didn't blame Terrence for that. There are ways for homeless men to find beds for the night and showers, but as far as I knew, there were no official funds in the city of Portland for weapons maintenance for the disenfranchised.

I tested the knife's edge on my thumb and drew an S shape of blood. Very thin, very accurate. Even Dad would've approved.

The question was, what was I supposed to do with it?

Jojo banged on the bathroom door. "Hey, Noah, the fuzz is here. They wanna take your statement."

"Be right out."

Great. The fuzz. I should hand the knife over to them. But after hearing the shot from a policeman's gun and watching Terrence crumple, I didn't trust them. Besides, Terrence had given the knife to me. I didn't know if he was going to live or die, but I'd made him a promise. I'd told him he could rest now, that I'd take over his job guarding the city.

I set the thing in the potpourri basket, took off my jacket, and scrubbed my arms until the skin looked like the desert, all dry and cracked. I changed into my new shirt, stole one of Jojo's fingertip towels, wrapped the knife in it, strapped it to my forearm with yards and yards of scratchy medical tape, and put my jacket back on.

I'd keep it for now.

When I came out to the Maxi Pad, another fight was going on. The glaring kind, between Jojo and some guy in a uniform with lots of gold gewgaws, gray military-cut hair, and no weapon holster. He was all fake seriousness, like Sonia's dad, the Appliance King. He looked like some puffed-up white guy whose job it was to shake the hands of other puffed-up white guys.

I touched my sleeve to make sure the blade couldn't slip out.

". . . for the unfortunate way in which this situation was handled," the serious guy was saying. "A thorough investigation will be conducted. That's why we need your help."

"You're gonna throw that pig in the slammer, I hope," Jojo said from the couch, where he was sitting next to Jaime. Jaime was picking dried blood from under her nails. *Good luck*, I thought. *That kind of stain doesn't come out.*

"That *pig* just turned twenty," the uniform said. "He's been suspended pending the results of our investigation."

Jojo huffed. "*Shyeah*, right. You're just gonna cover it up, aren't you? That man you shot was a veteran of a really crappy war. He was in the Hanoi Hilton, for god's sake. He deserves better."

"We're looking into it, sir," the police guy said, flashing a fake smile with lots of teeth. He looked like a skull. "That's why we're here."

"What I don't understand is why they were hassling him to begin with. He wasn't hurting anyone," Crock said. He was leaning against the kitchen counter, slurping a Fresca.

Flattop said, "We'd received complaints from a prominent member of the business community that he was loitering. Obstructing customers."

"Wait, you got complaints from the Fish Grotto?" Sonia said. "That can't be right. Terrence has been sitting there for months. Everyone knows he's harmless. Sometimes the waitresses give him leftover fries at the end of their shifts." She turned to Jojo. "Who owns the Fish Grotto, anyway?"

I felt tendrils of black smoke reaching out for me, beginning with the fine hairs at the nape of my neck.

"Not the Fish Grotto," I said, understanding. "The PfefferBrau Haus. Jurgen Pfeffer called you, didn't he?"

Everyone looked at me like I'd just magically appeared in their midst. A starman, beamed down from another world.

The guy in the uniform and flattop narrowed his eyes in an expression I recognized: *Oh yeah. You're that kid. The one whose dad blew his brains out.*

And then another man, one I hadn't seen at first, stood up from the table and made his way over to me.

I didn't know what Idiot Willy was doing here, since he was a member of the Gresham Police Department, not Portland's. Backup, maybe.

I was still glad to see him. He had the same huge pores as always, same Wild West mustache. His smile was weak but sincere. "I'm glad you're okay, Noah. When Crock told me what happened, I was afraid someone might've gotten you this time."

The decorated pig, I mean *policeman*, coughed subtly into his sleeve.

"This is Deputy Chief Simmons," Willy went on. "He's here to take your statements. It seems your boss here has taken issue with the handling of the situation." He jutted his chin toward the sofa.

Boss? *Jojo?*

Well, yeah, he did pay us for minding the store for him, so I guess that made him our boss.

I told Willy, "A man was shot in front of us. By a policeman. You can't expect us to be levelheaded."

Deputy Chief Simmons didn't say a word.

Idiot Willy nodded toward the table, where Evan was still pushing around his food. "Come on, Noah. Have a seat. Tell me what you saw. I promise to do my best to see justice is done."

I remembered him handing me a foam cup of coffee on the worst day of my life, and I followed him.

We sat at Jojo's Formica table, still loaded with cartons of cold lo mein and dumplings, and little plastic packets of sweet orange sauce.

Idiot Willy reached for a can of Fresca in the middle of the table, popped the tab, and slid it over to me.

I wrapped my hands around it. It wasn't even cold. "I don't know how much they've already told you. The fight started before we showed up. We were just trying to help."

Evan pushed the cabbage around his plate a little more loudly. *Stab!* went the chopsticks.

Idiot Willy cleared his throat. "Go on."

"Did they tell you that Terrence was really upset about something? That he kept saying, 'Keep her safe' and 'He's on the prowl'? He didn't say who, but he spent almost as much time around the PfefferBrau Haus as he did by the Fish Grotto. That's why I asked you about Pfeffer. I mean, is it possible Terrence saw Pfeffer do something? Maybe that's why Pfeffer complained about him? To get him out of the way?"

Deputy Chief Simmons was not smiling now. "That's a serious accusation." I had a feeling it wouldn't be nearly so serious if Herr Sick Freak Pfeffer wasn't such a prominent member of the business community.

"How serious?" Evan said. "I mean, we know for sure at least one girl turned up dead in their vat. Doesn't seem like such a stretch to me."

For a while nothing moved. Not even the air.

"Well?" I said.

You could see Deputy Chief Simmons trying to come up with an appropriate response. He finally said, "The individual you're talking about was acquitted in a court of law."

"We need to face facts, Noah," Idiot Willy said. "And the fact is that while Terrence is a decorated veteran, he also has a history of schizophrenia. *He sees things that aren't there.*" He stared at me as if he were sending me an encoded message. "Do you understand? Even if he thinks he saw something, who's to say it's real?"

"Just because you're paranoid doesn't mean they aren't out to get you," Evan mumbled.

"Pardon?" Idiot Willy said.

Evan unhooked a slogan button from his T-shirt and tossed it to us. It was a simple design—white words on a black background. The same words Evan just quoted.

"Even if Terrence is schizo, who's to say he's wrong?" Ev said.

"A judge. A jury. A mental health care professional," Simmons said.

I was getting real tired of this guy. Not tired enough to call him a pig to his face, but I definitely wanted him out of the Maxi Pad.

"You mean nobody's going to listen to him just because he's ill?" Jay's eyes narrowed. "Nobody's going to stand up for him for something that isn't his fault?"

"It's not as simple as that, miss—" Simmons started to say, but Jaime wasn't listening.

"I've had enough." She ran into the bathroom. Sonia was right behind her, ready to do whatever girls did in bathrooms when one of them was having a meltdown. Something with hugging and maybe mascara.

Jaime's little display sent Jojo into a fury. He clenched his fists, stood up, and took two steps toward Simmons before Crock got between them. "Don't," Crock said. "It's bad enough that Terrence is in the hospital. We don't want to have to bail you out."

"What am I supposed to do, man? I'm pissed off and way too old to be putting daisies in guns."

Crock said, "You could litigate. That's why the deputy chief is here, isn't he? There was some wrongful something or other?"

"Do I look like the kind of guy who has a lawyer, man?" Jojo said.

"Maybe not," Crock said. "But you remember freedom of speech, don't you? There's always the media."

Simmons shot a glare at Idiot Willy as if to say, *He's your stepson. Can't you keep him under control?*

It was Jojo's turn to smile in a way that showed too many teeth. "Oh, yeah," he said. "And the ACLU. And the *Oregonian*. If I were you, Deputy Chief Piggy—oink oink—I would make sure the best doctors are operating on Terrence. And that you've got a flak jacket on, 'cause I'm about to unleash one hell of a shitstorm."

While this was going on in the living area, Idiot Willy leaned over to me and whispered, "Do you trust me, son?"

And even though I didn't want to provoke anyone today, I couldn't help saying, "Duh."

He led me out onto the landing, closing the door behind him.

He looked through the frosted glass pane into the apartment, probably to make sure no one would come storming out to bother us. He said under his breath, "Get the girls home and keep them there. Do you understand? Lock the doors. Barricade them in if you have to. I *know* you know how to do that."

"So you believe Terrence," I said. "You think another girl is going to disappear."

For a moment his face seemed to crumble, like a piece of Jojo's ceiling. "Officially I can't comment. Let's just say the only thing worse than kids covered in blood is no kids at all," he said.

And that was it. I could no longer think of him as *Idiot* Willy.

"Lieutenant MacInnes . . ." I began.

"*Will* is fine, Noah."

"I'll take care of those two," I said, nodding toward the Maxi Pad. He knew who I meant. "But what about the rest? It's a big city."

He breathed so hard I was afraid he'd have a coronary. "That's our job." The worry showed in the creases around his eyes. "If you think of anything else—anything at all—call me, okay?"

And he grasped my forearm, the one with the knife in it.

I don't know how much he could feel through the layers of leather and towel, but he knew something was there, because he slid his fingers away.

Maybe he didn't know that it was Terrence's knife. Then again, maybe he did. He was a smart guy—definitely not an idiot.

He opened the door to the Maxi Pad. "Anything at all," he repeated, and he went back to put on his official law enforcement face.

When I was alone on the landing, I flashed back to my sister, in her nightshirt, standing in the living room so many years ago, too scared to be bossy, while I ran around the house lobbing Dad's stuff out on the lawn.

That was why Willy let me keep the knife. He was trying to tell me that I had to be ready for another siege. And this time, I had to win.

17

WE PRACTICED UNTIL ONE O'CLOCK, which in some ways wasn't late at all, but in others was way too late. Everyone looked battle-weary. Ev, Crock, and I insisted on following Jaime's car back to Gresham, and one of us walked each of the girls to the door. Neither of their dads was pleased to see us with their little girls, but there seemed to be a slight softening in Mr. Krajicek's expression, and Mr. Deleuze looked as though he were about to chew me out, when he looked at my feet. "Those look like solid boots, son." "They are, sir. Plenty." "Use them, Noah. And don't hold back."

Crock and I deposited Ev at his house at the top of Walter's Hill, then skulked back down to our own cul-de-sac.

Crock walked across the street back to his place, where he was probably jerking off to pictures of the female cast of *Dynasty*.

It was time for me to violate Dad's inner sanctum.

It wasn't like I never went in the garage anymore. I was there all the time. Dad may have been gone, but our house still had toilets that needed plunging, fridges that needed fixing, a lawn that needed mowing. But it was still his garage. Everything in it was his. And tonight I definitely needed *his* tools to clean Terrence's knife. Whether Terrence lived or died was out of my control. But at least I could take care of his stuff.

Dad had been the kind of guy with a wall of particleboard and chalk outlines where each screwdriver, each hammer, each handsaw was supposed to hang. Which made it easy to see exactly what he'd left me to work with.

It was also creepy, because they made the wall look like a crime scene and the tools look like corpses. And the spaces that were empty? The ones where his guns used to be? I tried to ignore the two empty outlines every time I came in, but I never could. They freaked me out every time.

Two missing weapons. Why was it always two? I toted up more pairs in my life: Sonia and me. Evan and me. Sonia and Jaime.

Then I imagined Jaime and me.

No. I'd had this argument with Evan years ago, after that game of Mafia in the seventh grade. He said Jaime should be the last victim. I'd told him he was an idiot and that Sonia was the prize. And hey, look at how well that turned out.

There was only one way to think of her. Jaime was an Old Girl. The one we all hung out with but nobody wanted to date. Too much history, I guess. Like when we were sophomores and she used the words "tubular" and "gnarly" in a way that made me gnash my teeth, like she was trying to be a Valley Girl. I mean, if you have to imitate a trend, why pick one that was so annoying?

All this was going through my mind as I found Dad's toolbox. There was a full can of WD-40 in it. I took off my jacket and ripped the knife off my arm, taking cuffs of arm hair with the medical tape. *Yow!*

I laid down an old rag on his tool bench and put the knife on it. I sprayed and rubbed it the way Dad had told me to. It was slow going, because my green hair kept getting in my eyes. I hadn't sprayed it into a mohawk in weeks, and it was so long it flopped around a lot.

As I worked, I found myself thinking more and more about Jaime, how she'd looked this afternoon with her arms dripping red, and the way she'd let Evan lean on her even though she looked like she was also about to topple over.

Jaime had stupid hair. But I thought about the short side of it, the way it looked over her ear, and how it made her neck look longer. I wondered what it would feel like running my lips up the length of that neck. Did she have a ticklish spot at the top of her spine? Would she shiver if I lightly ran my tongue from her shoulder blades to her hairline?

It didn't matter. She was leaving me. Just like Evan, she was going to some college on the other side of the country in a few months. I'd have to find a girlfriend from the remaining local herd, which was getting picked off, one by one.

The world was going to shit, and once again all I could do was clean.

I don't know how much later it was when I looked down and realized that my work was done. Terrence's blade wasn't just clean; it shone like platinum. You could grip the rubber handle and it stayed gripped, not slippery with eons of sweat and grime and Jack Daniels and probably human pee.

I had a split second to think, *I need to test this on something*, when I grabbed a handful of my green hair, yanked it straight up, and mowed it like an overgrown lawn. I looked at the piles of it on the floor around me. The color looked toxic. What if that dye had leaked into my brain?

"Jesus Christ, nimrod, what the hell are you doing?"

Cilla stood at the entrance to the garage, wearing her beige zip-up uniform and sensible waitressing shoes. She took in the whole scene—the lights, the workbench, the chalk outlines we'd never bothered to erase, the remains of my hair on the ground all around me, the knife in my hand.

Of all the times in my life I must've looked like a dangerous wacko, this had to be the worst.

I was too tired to tell her the whole stupid story of the

day, and how I'd come to be here. Instead, I said the first thing that came to my mind: "I was thinking about a girl."

Time seemed to slow. The light over Dad's workbench gave a zzzt sound. To me it sounded like craZZZy craZZZy craZZZy.

Cilla stared at me. "A girl."

I nodded.

"Not Sonia?"

I shook my head.

Her expression didn't change. "I take it this girl doesn't like guys with mohawks."

"I don't know," I said. "I figured it was worth a try."

She reached out, took the knife from me, and jammed it onto one of Dad's pegs. It didn't quite fit. Dad was going to kill us.

Wait—no he wasn't.

I was about to clean up the mess when Cilla pulled the chain that turned off the tubular workbench light and linked her arm in mine. "Come on. Let's fix your hatchet job."

She led me upstairs to our Jack and Jill bathroom, opened a drawer marked CILLA'S! KEEP OUT!, and unrolled a small rug with slim compartments for different scissors. She ran her fingers over each of them, selecting just the right one. She snipped and cut and snipped and cut. While she worked, she bit her lip a lot, and said things like, "Maybe a little more from this side." Didn't give me a lot of confidence.

But it didn't matter. Cilla was running her fingers through my hair again, the way she used to when she sang me to sleep.

"Well?" she said when she was done. "Whaddya think?"

I looked at my reflection in the mirror. She'd made my black hair spiky-short all over, like I'd gotten an electric shock. I still had the bull's-eye T-shirt and the dog collar. The scar on my nose was red but already starting to fade.

Let me make one thing clear: I still wasn't handsome. I wasn't Bowie material. But for the first time ever, I liked what I saw.

"Well?" she said again, waiting for a compliment.

I leaned in closer, looking for flaws. There were plenty. Was that a zit or an ingrown hair on my jaw? But the biggest flaw, the one I didn't know I'd been looking for, I didn't find.

"I don't look like Dad," I said.

She put her hand on my shoulder and her eyes met mine in the mirror. "Is that why you've been doing this punk thing? You've been afraid you'd look like *him*?"

"Duh," I said.

Cilla shook her head. "You're not him, Noah. You could never be him."

"How can you say that? After I pushed you?"

"I thought about it a lot, Noah. I've been pushing you for years in little ways. Expecting you to blow. And it wasn't right. Everyone gets mad sometimes, little bro.

You can't go through life never getting angry. I see how hard you try. You come home stitched up, your jacket covered in blood . . ."

"You saw that?"

"Shut up, nimrod. We're having a moment." She whacked me on the head with a pair of scissors. "Where was I? Oh yeah. All these years. You've never tried to hurt anyone. I've seen you come back from clubs bruised and bloody. But it was always about you, Noah. You deliberately went to places where you hurt yourself again and again."

I only knew Cilla was uncomfortable because she threw her hairdressing scissors into the tub without sweeping up the green hair first. This was hard for her to admit.

It was hard for me too. No one ever wants to know your older sister is right.

"*That's* why you're not Dad. Got nothing to do with your hair. I worry about you plenty, but never—not once—because I thought you'd turn out like him." She looked at her watch. "It's two thirty in the morning. I'm going to bed. But keep looking at yourself in the mirror, Noah. Remind yourself what you see."

It was only later I realized she had called me by my name. Not "nimrod" or "idiot."

Noah. That was the closest my sister ever got to telling me she loved me.

• • •

Hours later, just after I finally fell asleep, I woke to catch the smell of Marlboros stinking up my space.

I hoisted myself up on my elbows. Ziggy was sitting at my desk, legs loosely crossed.

"It's happening again."

After the shock of seeing him in my bedroom wore off, I remembered I was mad at him. "Where the hell did you disappear to yesterday afternoon?"

"I'm here to help you fight the Marr, son. I have no power over stupidity."

He was talking about the jumpy police kid with the gun.

It was a crap answer, and to make it worse he flicked ash onto my carpet.

"Do you mind? Some of us have to live here."

He took another drag. "You need to focus on the real problem."

"Which is what?" I said. "'Cause I'm losing count of what I'm supposed to be worrying about." I ticked them off on my fingers. "There's Terrence, who got shot in the chest. There's every teenage girl in the city. Oh yeah, and then there's Evan, who keeps popping pills and gets skinnier each day. Have I left anything out?"

He leaned forward and steepled his fingers. His crooked teeth glowed so much I thought they might have a half-life. "There's a pattern, old boy. You can feel it, can't you? You just haven't put it together yet. Terrence was close. That's why he went down. He tried to tell you."

I lay back. "Listen, man. I'm tired. I spent half the day up to my elbows in gore. Can't you please let me sleep? I promise I'll think when I get up."

I turned my head to the wall and folded the pillow over my ears. I didn't know how he got in and out of places, but I was hoping that if I ignored him he'd disappear. Glimmer off somewhere else.

He didn't. I knew he didn't because the smoke got closer to my head.

"You can't escape me. The more you try to shake me off, the more I'll be with you."

The burn was quick and unexpected. A cigarette stubbed out on my right hand, in the valley between my thumb and forefinger.

I screamed. Ziggy leaned in closer and whispered, "It shouldn't have to be this way, Noah. Use your ears. Use your eyes. Find a way to understand things other than through pain."

Of course Mom and Cilla came running, but as soon as they flicked on the lights, Ziggy was gone.

18

"MY GOD, NOAH! WHAT HAVE YOU DONE TO YOURSELF?"

Mom had my hand in hers. There was a smoking crater in the valley between my thumb and forefinger.

"Smoking. In bed. Fell asleep."

Cilla came running back in with a bag of frozen peas for my burning hand and tucked me in bed. My sheets were midnight blue with glow-in-the-dark constellations on the pillowcases. So as soon as Mom and Cilla flipped off my bedroom light, I felt like I was lying in a field of stars. My room was cold but peaceful. If it wasn't for my throbbing hand, it would've been easy to float away into the stratosphere.

There was another reason I couldn't get to sleep right away. Mom and Cilla left the door cracked, probably to keep an eye on me. So I heard them shushing each other in the hall and saw silhouettes of fingers pressed to lips. They might as well have yelled, "WE WANT TO TALK ABOUT YOU AND IT ISN'T GOING TO BE GOOD!"

So of course I had to listen.

Good thing I was an expert at playing possum, another skill I'd learned from living with Dad. I could always tell by the lurch and creep of his shadow, the way it reached and coiled like smoke, when he was coming for someone—anyone—to leave his permanent mark on.

On those nights there was nothing to do but play dead.

Nope. Nothing here. Just a pile of sleeping kid under covers the color of the midnight sky.

That skill served me now. Mom and Cilla thought I was asleep after only a minute.

Mom said, "Let me get this straight, honey. You think he's deliberately hurting himself?"

"You saw the burn, Mom. That was more than just random ash. Someone ground it out on his hand. Hard. And he was the only one in the room."

"Couldn't someone else have done it? Maybe he's hiding Sonia in there somewhere. He's always been a sucker for her. Goddamn. I *knew* we should've pressed charges after what she did to his nose."

I heard Cilla huff. She loved knowing more than other people. "Sonia's over, Mom."

"How do you know?"

"Oh, please. She scarred him for life. Noah may be clueless but he's not stupid."

"Have you seen his personal finance grades? He can be very stupid."

"Well, yeah, I suppose so," Cilla said. "But not about Sonia. Not anymore. Earlier tonight, when I cut his hair, he said he was interested in someone new."

Silence. I could practically hear Mom chewing her lip, like she did when she couldn't make something add up.

"So that's it, then. He did this to himself. Why? Is he really that desperate for attention?"

"I don't understand it either," Cilla said. "This band thing has made him a little loopy. It's almost like he won't let himself be happy. Like something's dragging him back."

Mom swore in a way she would never have dared when Dad was alive.

". . . asshole still screwing with us after all these years. I knew I should've gotten Noah into therapy. Or medicated him. But he seemed fine."

"He had Evan."

Mom sighed. "No kidding. I don't know what Noah would do without him."

And that was the problem. I didn't either.

A week went by and March turned to April. Didn't make much difference in the weather. Either it was rainy and gray, like in Gresham, or rainy and gray and stinking of hops, like in Portland. The whole sprawl seemed depressing and industrial—a city of old bridges and warehouses and unused train tracks that led into brick walls.

The PfefferFest was in two weeks, but we still hadn't heard from the Pfeffer brothers about who was in the lineup. There were teaser posters all around town, though: *PfefferFest. Who Will It Be?* With a dotted outline of a random head and shoulders. Drove us nuts. Crock tugged hard on clumps of his hair. Not only did *not knowing* not jive with his control freak nature, he was getting interrogated daily from us.

"Honestly, how soon until we find out?" Evan said one afternoon in my Gremlin on the way to the Maxi Pad. He was riding shotgun, as usual, and Crock was in back. People stared at Ev's rainbow dreads at every stoplight. It was like driving a motorized fishbowl.

"I don't know," Crock told him. "Look, the fact that we haven't heard is good news. A bunch of bands have already gotten flushed. We're probably in the top thirty."

"Out of how many?"

Crock fake-coughed. "One hundred seventy-two," he said.

Ev sighed and pinched the bridge of his nose. "Jesus, that's a lot," he said.

Crock said, "I don't know how word got out, but it did. There were even bands from Austin, Texas. Everyone wants a big break."

"I had no idea the odds were that bad," Ev said. "This changes everything."

"Like what?" I said. "What does it change?"

Ev looked out the window, flipped off the latest carful of people who were staring at his hair, and said, "It makes a difference in how I can keep getting away. I told Dad we were rehearsing for the PfefferFest."

"Is that it?" I said. "You're worried about excuses? Take it easy, then. If this falls through, Crock'll get us another gig. Right, Crock?"

"No prob," Crock said. "We'll find something sooner or later."

Evan slouched in his seat. "Sooner would be better," he said.

In that dead calm of the next week, Crock kept a chore chart taped to the door in the Maxi Pad with everyone's name and their work rotation. To get us off his back when we weren't practicing, he said. Dinner. Store. Dishes. Terrence.

Terrence the Homeless Knife-Wielding Vet had survived the operation to remove the bullet and fix the internal damage. But his rehab was a bitch. The doctors thought he might've had a small stroke at some point. All we knew was that, because of either the stroke or a lot of Thorazine, the guy was a drooling idiot. One of us visited him at Emanuel Hospital every afternoon, but after he got all the tubes out, not a lot changed. Someone kept the TV on in his room all the time, but he didn't watch it. Instead, he spent hours staring at the giant mutant rhododendron outside his window.

I liked pulling the Terrence shift and often swapped Maxi Pad chores so I could spend more time with him. I found it restful talking to a guy who didn't talk back. I told him everything. I told him about my dad and what it had been like cleaning his head off the basement wall. I told him about Ziggy and the Marr. I told him how worried I was about Evan.

Each time, I brought Terrence's knife with me. Each time, I looked for a way to give it back to him. Each time, I decided it was a bad idea. Until one afternoon, when the door to the hall was closed and I was strumming tunes on my acoustic guitar. I told him I thought the Marr might also have something to do with the Disappearing Girls.

"I just don't understand, Terrence," I said. *Strum strum strum.* "There's got to be a pattern. I know it. Willy's working on it, but I don't think whoever's taking these girls will slip up again anytime soon. He's too good." I paused to tune up. "I still think it has something to do with the PfefferBrau Haus."

I put the pick in my mouth and tightened up my G string. Then I looked up. Terrence was staring at me, his eyes completely focused. There was no drool.

I put the guitar down and held the straw for his cranberry juice up to his mouth. He swatted it away.

"I believe you have something of mine," he said, as though he had never been sedated or on antipsychotics. I didn't know how he pulled it off, but he was even better at playing possum than I was.

He slipped a hand from under his blankets and beckoned for it. He even snapped his fingers. *Gimme.*

I reached into my jacket pocket but stopped. "Are you sure this is the right place to give it to you? Shouldn't you be discharged first?"

"Son, they ain't never gonna discharge me. As soon as I look better, they're shuffling me off to the psych ward. I heard them."

And now I had a decision. Was Terrence harmless? Or wasn't he? "If I give this to you, do you promise not to use it on any doctors or nurses? Or police guys or nuns?"

He snapped his fingers again. "You let me worry about that. You've got enough to worry about already."

I didn't kid myself. I knew what I was doing. I knew I'd smuggled a concealed weapon into a crowded hospital. I knew Terrence hadn't given me any guarantees. But I handed it over anyway, and his hand, now clean and white and flopping around like a cod, snatched it from me and slid it under his mattress.

I tried to guess how I'd feel if I found out later some orderly had had his throat cut because Terrence went on a rampage.

But I doubted he would. Even as he hid the knife, I had a feeling that the worst that would happen would be what actually did—that he'd bust out of the hospital, and the only casualties would be the window frame and the hundred-year-old rhododendron on the ground two stories below.

When I came back to the Maxi Pad that afternoon, I knew at once that everyone else was worried about something, and that it wasn't Terrence.

Ziggy was sitting on the open windowsill, flicking ash on the sidewalk below. He had a mean-dad look in his eyes, as if to say: *I warned you.*

Sonia, Crock, and Evan were clustered around Jojo's TV set. Sonia was sitting on the alpaca carpet, her long legs stretched in front of her. Crock was leaning forward on the sofa, his fingers steepled, like he was part of an important meeting. Ev was sitting next to him. His bass was in his hands but he wasn't playing.

"'S goin' on?" I said, dumping my guitar case by the door.

Sonia shushed me and went back to watching.

I came closer to see what they were so interested in. It wasn't MTV, or reruns of *Gilligan's Island.*

No. They were watching the news. The *news.* Reporters in trench coats with perfect hair, standing on blustery Portland streets.

It didn't take me long to figure out what that meant.

Terrence had been right. Pfeffer had done it again.

• • •

Her name was Tracy del Campo. She was a junior at Madison High School. Her parents were from El Salvador, but Tracy was born in Portland. According to interviews with her hollow-eyed parents, Tracy wanted to be a social worker, to help people like them—the kind with heavy accents—get used to how things worked in the United States.

Tracy had been coming home from her internship at a legal aid office on Fremont Street. She was last seen at a TriMet bus stop on the corner of Fremont and Thirty-ninth. Nobody saw her get on the bus. Nobody saw her get into a car with some psycho either. She just . . . disappeared.

By now there had been so many missing girls, the police pounced right away, and so did the media. The whole city wanted her back *now*.

So reporters interviewed her family. They interviewed her classmates. They interviewed the police. Everyone kept repeating her name. *Tracy. Tracy. Tracy.* The message was: *We did not raise this child to be a victim. Let her go, whoever you are, you sick freak.*

They kept showing pictures of her: in a prom dress leaning into a date who was shorter than she was, holding a gaudy debate trophy, looking to the side in front of some splattered blue photography-studio backdrop. Her black hair looked like it had been cut with blunt gardening shears, and she had a skinny rattail of a braid snaking down her back.

Wait, a rattail?

"She looks like . . ."

Ev bounded up from the sofa before I could say any more, grabbed my arm, and pulled me out of the apartment and onto the landing.

He hissed at me: "Jesus Christ, Noah! Sonia's already freaked enough. Do you want to freak her out more?" He did a back-check into the Maxi Pad to see if anyone was watching us.

The last time we'd talked about the girls on the Disappearing Wall at Denny's, he'd told me there was no pattern, that I'd go nuts trying to find one.

"Ha!" I said. "Ha ha *ha*! So I'm not crazy. You see it too!"

Evan wrinkled his nose at me like I smelled like Terrence sitting in a dumpster on a hot summer day. He was disgusted. "Believe it or not, Noah, not everything's about *you*."

Then I noticed his eye. It was half closed, like something was pressing on it.

"Ev, do you need your headache meds?"

He huffed. "Go help Jaime in the store."

He went back into the Maxi Pad and slammed the door behind him. The frosted glass rattled but held firm.

Jojo was gone when I came in the store, and Jaime had a line of customers ten deep.

We didn't have time to talk to each other until we closed. The loudspeakers were off; Jaime was counting out the till, and I was wiping down the front case with Windex and a paper towel.

I realized I hadn't talked to Jaime since Terrence got shot. When we weren't rehearsing, Crock kept our chore rotations pretty far apart and his closer to hers. We'd all seen him try to flirt with her, but she seemed too tired to do anything about it. At least before Evan smacked Crock upside the head and reminded him the Old Girls were off-limits, no exceptions.

Now I noticed the bags under Jaime's eyes, and remembered the sound of a gunshot, and crouching on the sidewalk, and then Jaime, her bloody arms like satin gloves. It almost didn't matter that Terrence was recovering. You never forget seeing up close what a bullet can do when it tears through human flesh.

"You did good the other day. With Terrence," I said. "If it hadn't been for you, he might not've pulled through."

She wouldn't look at me. "I've been trying to figure out how to tell you." Her eyes flicked up to mine, then back to the piles of dimes and quarters. "My parents don't want me hanging out here anymore. They let me come today to say good-bye to Jojo. Starting tomorrow I have to stay home and study after school."

Crap. As Idiot Willy would say, it was *that woman* again.

"You mean they don't want you hanging out with *us*," I said. She kept re-counting change—because she screwed up the count each time, or she didn't want to look up. "Or is it just me?" She closed her eyes. She didn't say anything. "They think I'm trouble."

"'Troubled' was the word they used. Trouble with a 'd.'"

"It's okay," I said. "I understand."

"They're wrong," she said softly, almost as if she hadn't said anything at all. "They don't hear you, Noah. They don't know the work you've been doing. Even if they did hear it, they wouldn't understand."

She was so upset I just meant to hug her, but it didn't work out that way. Instead, I lifted her chin so she'd look up at me and I brushed her lips with mine. "Don't worry," I said. "We'll find a way."

And I kissed her again.

She'd said her parents hadn't heard us play. She'd said that even if they had, they wouldn't appreciate what we were trying to do.

In that still moment I heard the sizzle of the neon sign outside where the second J in JOJO'S RECORDS kept shorting out. I heard Sonia banging the crap out of the floor tom upstairs and felt sorry for Castaneda the goldfish. I heard the scratching of a record on a turntable where we'd forgotten to take the needle off.

I heard the softest brushing of wings over our heads.

I don't know how we know the things we do. Maybe, like Jojo thinks, there is a higher plane of existence that you can reach by feeding pot to a goldfish. Or maybe, like Terrence, you can smell danger and protect yourself and the city you love with a hunting blade and a tinfoil hat.

Or maybe, if you're like me, you have to suss it out bit by bit, note by note, until you understand that you've made art and it doesn't matter what anyone else thinks.

Because that was how that moment between Jaime and me felt. Something that only the two of us could hear and feel.

I loved how, in that moment, everything else fell away. Even as I was kissing her, I knew that moments like this didn't come often, so I memorized each beat of it.

I memorized the way I wiped her eyes with my calloused thumbs. I memorized the gloss on her lips and how they tasted like strawberries.

I memorized the way her curly hair felt under my fingers, and that while I would've expected that much perm to feel fried, the hair itself felt soft and smooth.

I memorized how, when I brushed her forehead with my lips, the darkness around us didn't seem so deep.

I knew then what made her an Old Girl, and it had nothing to do with what she wore or who she hung out with, and everything to do with who she *was*. Jaime was the girl who gave you the shirt off her back when your nose was ripped up.

I had lifted her sweater high enough that I could feel the soft skin around her waist, when she broke away.

Too fast? I thought.

Then I saw what she saw.

Evan was standing at the back door. He did not look happy.

"I came to tell you that Crock just got the call. We're number two on the call sheet for the PfefferFest. The only ones higher are the Crazy 8s."

He turned away and slammed the door behind him.

Slowly, the hops smell crept into the store again.

I ran after Ev but turned back to take one last look at Jaime. She nodded.

We'd had our moment.

Now I had to deal with the Marr.

19

THE TEMPERATURE IN THE STORE dropped twenty degrees. Outside the night grew deeper, as if something had swallowed the stars.

Noah, I heard the Marr hiss. *Relaxxx. I'm not coming for you.*

I bolted up the stairs to the Maxi Pad. I didn't see Jojo or Ziggy, and I definitely didn't see Ev. His messenger bag lay in a heap by the front door, but Ev himself was nowhere to be found.

Sonia was gleefully chopping vegetables next to a sizzling wok. Crock was talking on the wall phone with the twisty cord. A big smile wrapped his face. They were still high from the news, clueless about what was coming.

I took a deep breath and exhaled frosty bile.

Outside the darkness hissed: *Soon he'll be all mine.* I leaned out the window over the street by the Fish Grotto.

No Ev below. I looked up the street to the PfefferBrau Haus. Starting at the brewery, streetlights winked out one by one.

Part of me is already inssside him.

It was coming.

I slammed the window down and ran around the Maxi Pad, closing the rest of them. *Slam!* Lock. *Slam!* Lock. Time to get us ready for a siege.

Crock saw me and hung up the phone. He walked toward me with his arms open like he expected me to run into them. "Did you hear the great news? Number two on the call sheet! Isn't that awesome? What's the matter, man? You don't look too good."

Gnawing my way out as we ssspeak.

"I'm fine." *Slam!* Lock. "Where's Ev? Is he in the bathroom?"

Sonia turned around. "Isn't he with you guys? He went downstairs to tell you and Jaime . . ." Her eyes narrowed. She looked at her watch. "Wait—what were you and Jaime doing alone down there? The store closed a half hour ago."

She pointed a sharp paring knife at me, but I didn't care. If she was pissed she could have my other nostril. Shit, she could have my whole face. Just not right now. "You'll have to ask *her*. I've gotta find Ev."

I felt Ziggy before I saw him. He was at my right shoulder. Always on my right. He whispered: "Quickly, Noah. The alley. He's still out there." Right. The alley. How could

I have forgotten? "The bag, son. Bring the bag! He may need it!"

I plucked Evan's messenger bag from its spot by the door and followed Ziggy down the stairs, vaulting them three at a time.

The back exit from the store not only led to the cat pee stairwell, it led to a solid-metal outside door, so rusted and repainted and warped with age we practically needed a linebacker to slam it all the way closed. We used it to take out the trash.

I didn't stop at the bottom of the stairs but used the momentum to ram into it. Stuck. I should've known. I shouldered it open and stumbled into the inky night.

I found Ev gripping the lip of the dumpster, both his eyes screwed tight, massaging his temple with his free hand. The world's biggest thunderhead was closing in on him, reaching, curling, and uncurling. It was cold. Oh, so cold. And it whispered.

Sooo young. Sssuch talent. He's delicious.

I reached to pry Ev's grip off the dumpster. "Come on, man. We've gotta get you outta here." I pushed his messenger bag behind my back to get a better hold on Ev's scrawny arms.

Ev swatted me away. "No Old Girls! We promised! That was the deal!"

His right eye was really twitching now. Was he having a seizure? "Now's not the time, Ev. We gotta go."

"After Sonia I thought you'd learn! We agreed it was hands off! We had a pact!"

Can you hear him pop? Can you hear him explode?

The Marr was inching closer, the darkness consuming everything in its path. It didn't come straight ahead like it was walking. It was sneakier than that. It would curl over something, say an empty bottle of Jack Daniels (this *was* an alley), as though it were tasting it, then retreat for a second or two, which made me think it would let that thing alone, only to come back stronger and swallow it whole.

"Pact!" Evan was still shouting at me, but I was only half paying attention to him.

"Whatever. I'm an asshole. Let's finish this conversation inside."

He shook me off. "Mafia, Noah. Remember Mafia? She was supposed to be the last one to die!"

I finally suctioned him from the dumpster. "Nobody's dying here. Not tonight."

I draped his arm around my shoulder and half carried, half dragged him back to the Maxi Pad entrance.

I rattled the doorknob. Shit! It was stuck. I kicked it. Hard. It wouldn't give.

What now? Stand here and shout upstairs, hoping that someone would hear me and let us in? I'd just closed all the windows.

You know where I started? Where would it cause him the most pain?

Zzzt. Another, closer streetlight flickered out.

I felt chills in places I normally didn't get chilled. My knees. My thumbs.

Ev's whole body was racked by shivers.

I searched the street, looking for an escape, and saw a yellow halo the Marr hadn't reached. It was on the corner. A head of golden hair atop a golden suit. He sparkled like an award. "Too late, Noah! You'll have to run for it!" Ziggy said. "Where are your car keys?"

I patted my jacket pocket and got a reassuring jangle.

"Come on, then, son. Move it!" He motioned us toward him, unusually frantic.

"Right. Ev, let's get you home."

You can't get him away in time.

I zigzagged us down the block. He wasn't that heavy—he just wasn't helping. Dead weight draped over my shoulder, like a really heavy leather jacket.

"All the girls," Evan said, then grunted. "Why do you have to have all the girls?"

The Marr was closing in. I could feel it pricking my heels even through my boots. Faster. I had to go faster.

Where the hell had I parked? Were the streets always this tangled?

But there was Ziggy's yellow head, always five paces ahead of us, always pointing where we needed to go next. "This way, Noah! Hurry!"

I kept looking over my shoulder. The third time I glanced back, I accidentally loosened my hold on Ev's arm. He dropped, a rolling ball of pain on the sidewalk.

The Marr was so close now I could feel its cold poison creeping through my veins, freezing me from my feet up.

I knelt over Ev. "Let me see your eye," I said.

He looked up. The whole right side of his face was twitching.

And that was when I knew.

We weren't going to outrun the Marr. Not this time.

I patted him on the shoulder. "You're fine, Ev. We'll have you home soon."

Then I stood and faced the black cloud that had been dogging us, and I smiled. If it was going to get Evan, it was going to get me too.

Let it come.

Here are some things I learned about the Marr from the inside:

1. It doesn't eat you up right away. It takes its time, snipping and jabbing at your flesh.
2. The unbearable pain Evan had been feeling? Inside that black cloud, I could feel it too. It was the worst I'd ever felt. And I knew pain. But the kind I knew was sharp and quick, like a gunshot. In this there was no hope of relief. It teased you for a moment, letting you go, thinking it was done, before coming in for another attack.
3. Bad as the pain was, the fear was worse. Ziggy was right. *Pop you like a balloon.* It whispered that we had

nothing to look forward to, so we should just lie down on the sidewalk right here and give up.

That last part pissed me off. The Marr was a bully. Just like my dad.

My eyes snapped open. I was hunched over Ev, wrapped around him, trying to protect him from the worst of it.

Give up? Curl up here in a heap? No way.

I stood over Evan and closed my eyes. I didn't expect to see anything. That wasn't the point. I never understood anything with my eyes. I had to hear things to believe them.

That was why I started strumming chords on my jeans. I knew what we needed. An anthem.

It didn't take long. I started humming the chorus. Just a tune—no lyrics, but to me it sounded like strength.

Nicccce try, Noah. But we both know you don't have brain one.

I let doubt creep into my voice. I faltered. I thought about lying down next to Evan. It would be so easy, like going to sleep.

That was when I felt the lightest of touches on my shoulder, and even though it was too dark to see him, I knew Ziggy was there. He had enough confidence for all three of us. Together, we hauled Evan up and finished the chorus.

I'm standing with you
We'll face it together
Don't be afraid
Never be afraid

I sang the chorus over and over again to give Evan courage. To give me courage.

Something must've worked, because when I opened my eyes the Marr was gone. It was still cold and dark and damp, but regular Northwest-in-April damp. We could still feel the pain, but it was fading, like the after-image of an explosion.

Ziggy, who I thought for sure would have disappeared, was still standing at my shoulder, his touch as light as feathers. He looked at me and smiled as a father would. A proud one.

Evan leaned into me. The right side of his face still looked as though it were melting off, but it was no longer twitching. "Not bad, Noah," he said. "What was that progression again?"

Slowly, the streetlights flickered on again, one by one, as though someone flipped a switch.

Together, Ev and I hobbled to my car, counterpoint to each other, with an icon of a man always five paces ahead of us, showing us the way home.

WHEN WE PULLED UP TO EV'S HOUSE on the hill later that night,
Mrs. Tillstrom was standing in the open doorway. She
did not look happy. Although it was tough to tell these
days if she was really mad or if it was just her eyebrows,
which she'd plucked into a high arch. She looked a little
like Cruella De Vil from *101 Dalmatians*. She looked as
though, if she could, she'd peel the skin from my back
and make a coat of it.

"I'll take it from here, Noah," Mrs. Tillstrom said, taking
Evan's arm from me. He lurched into her embrace.

I followed them to the family room at the back of the
house. It had floor-to-ceiling windows—the ones with
the view of five mountains in two states. Handy to watch
Mount St. Helens exploding the year before.

Yeah, the view was a bonus of living on a hillside. The
drawback? According to Ev, it was erosion. I never felt

it myself, but he said that after every rainstorm the floor seemed to be in a different place, so you never knew where you stood.

Mrs. Tillstrom lowered Ev onto the sofa and I pulled his boots off. He lay back while his mom smoothed his fried, dreaded hair away from his face. Meanwhile, I went into the kitchen and got a clean tea towel from the linens drawer, ran it under the cold tap, and brought it back in, careful not to drip water on the plush carpet. I'd spent so much time there I knew all the Tillstroms' "Evan's Sick" routines. We'd done it so much it was practically choreographed.

Not tonight. Cruella definitely wanted me gone. I could see it in the way she took the tea towel without looking at my face.

I wasn't sure what I'd done this time that she disapproved of. Here's a short list of possibilities:

1. I'd kept Evan out past six o'clock on a school night.
2. I'd brought him home sick.
3. I'm pretty sure we'd never paid her husband for all the times he'd sewed me up. But then again, we'd never gotten a bill.
4. Accessories. My mohawk was gone, my nose ring was gone, but I still wore a studded dog collar and leather jacket. Definitely not featured in all those fashion magazines she read.
5. Two words: wall bleaching.

While Mrs. Tillstrom sponged down Evan's forehead, I pulled giant pill bottles from his messenger bag and arranged them on the coffee table. There was Valium, Percocet (ninety count, refills = YES), and others whose names I didn't recognize but looked about the size of horse suppositories.

Dr. Tillstrom appeared: a lurching Scandinavian presence, glasses askew, carrying a cracked-leather doctor's bag.

"I wasn't sure which ones to give him," I said, pointing to the pill bottles.

Dr. Tillstrom ignored me. He sat on a footstool and pulled a blood pressure cuff and a stethoscope from his bag. "How bad was it this time, son?" he said.

"It's nothing, Dad."

"It's not *nothing*, Evan," Dr. Tillstrom said, inflating the blood pressure cuff around Ev's arm. "You have to take care of yourself. Health care is a partnership."

Mrs. Tillstrom smoothed Ev's hand with two carefully manicured fingers. She had to get fake nails every month because she chewed through the ones that God gave her at an alarming rate. ("You should see the real ones," Evan once told me. "They're all stunted and twisty and bleeding. They're worse than yours.")

With his family crowded around Evan, I wasn't sure of my next move. "Is there anything else you—"

"We'll take it from here, Noah," Mrs. Tillstrom said, still not looking at me. "You can go home now."

"Oh," I said. "Are you sure I can't—"

Mrs. Tillstrom whipped around. Definitely Cruella De Vil. For the first time, I noticed little broken blood vessels in the whites of her eyes. She was more than mad—she was barely keeping herself together.

"Go home, Noah. I'll forgive you tomorrow. I promise. Just not tonight. There's too much going on."

I shrugged. "No prob," I said, and turned to leave. I got about as far as the kitchen, then turned around. I don't know what stopped me, other than I was tired of being a free-floating asshole.

"Just out of curiosity, forgive me for what? This time, I mean."

"Shut up, Noah," Evan said before his dad thrust a thermometer under his tongue.

And that was when Mrs. Tillstrom blew like Mount St. Helens. "Oh, come on, Noah! It's not just tonight, and you know it." She stood up and poked me in the chest. "You know what he's been putting off and still you keep him out night after night, rehearsing for this stupid contest, which, aside from everything else, you won't be playing because *some girl was killed there!*"

"HE DOESN'T KNOW!" Evan yelled. He sat up. The thermometer went flying across the room in a shower of spit. I picked it up and rinsed it under the tap in the kitchen sink.

There were so many things I wanted to apologize for, so many things I wanted to ask. But I didn't, because they would only lead to a fight. And that's not what a good health partnership was about, apparently.

Mrs. Tillstrom was right. It was time for me to go.

"Right," I said, standing on the kitchen threshold. "See you tomorrow, Ev."

Mrs. Tillstrom had plopped herself in a Barcalounger and was staring at me with new interest.

"There's no way," she said. "Are you really that stupid, Noah?"

"He's not stupid," Ev said. "I never told him."

She stared at me again, taking in everything from my square-toed boots to my new spiky hair. But for the first time, possibly ever, I got the idea that she was trying to look behind all that, to see what I was really made of.

"How could you not know?" she said. "It's been three years. You two see each other every day."

"You mean that Evan's sick? He says it's migraines, but they started after his appendectomy, right? That's what's going on? He's having complications?"

Mrs. Tillstrom's eyes narrowed, like here was a problem she could finally get her brain around.

"Appendectomy?" Mrs. Tillstrom said. "*Appendectomy?* Evan still has his appendix, Noah. He just doesn't have a—"

"*Mom!*"

"Evan, honey, you swore up and down . . . Oh lord. I've gotten this all wrong." She pinched the bridge of her nose with two red dragon-lady fingers.

I was beginning to see why the Tillstroms hadn't had me to dinner in a while. I still didn't know exactly what was going on, but it had nothing to do with my green hair, and everything to do with Evan.

Evan said, "Can you blame me, Mom? It's embarrassing."

"It's not your fault," Dr. Tillstrom said, taking off the blood pressure cuff. "You have no reason to be ashamed. It sometimes happens this way. There's no logic to it."

"He's eighteen, Harald. Don't you remember what you were like when you were eighteen?" Mrs. Tillstrom said.

"Whether he's eighteen or not, he knows it's time. I'll call Dr. Rolfe. See if we can get you in, in the morning."

Evan's face got red and twisted. "So soon? Oh god, no. Please, Dad. I'm not ready."

"Not ready for what?" I said.

Evan turned his face away from all of us and sobbed into the back of the chintz sofa. I knew he was crying because of the way his shoulders moved and settled, then moved and settled a little lower. It was like watching him erode.

I felt a crack start to open between us then. The truth is, I didn't understand what I was seeing. Ever since Idiot Willy had covered the two of us with a blanket the afternoon my dad shot himself, it never occurred to me that Ev and me were two different people.

His parents watched their son cry but didn't move to comfort him. They seemed beyond comforting, and now they could only watch him twist and wreck himself.

"There are *masses* on his brain, Noah," Mrs. Tillstrom said. "They're affecting him. They need to come out before it spreads even more than it already has. Evan was supposed to have surgery a month ago, but he convinced us to wait until after you found out about the PfefferFest. We should've insisted way before this."

"It's not a big deal. Dr. Rolfe said at this point another month shouldn't make any difference," Evan said. He'd stopped twitching, but his voice was muffled by overstuffed cushions.

"Were you and I in the same consultation, Evan?" Dr. Tillstrom said. "Because what I heard was that the masses should come out right away, and then we'd see."

There was something the Tillstroms weren't saying. *Masses* was just a pretty word covering an ugly thing. Like Mrs. Tillstrom's fake nails.

"We got in," I said, not knowing if I should mention it or not. "We just found out today."

Dr. Tillstrom spared me a glance. "Yes, well, the point is moot, now, isn't it?" he said. "We can't put off this procedure any longer. You'll have to pull out or get another bassist."

"Another bassist?" I said stupidly.

Ev heaved harder. I wondered if the idea was just as repulsive to him as it was to me, because honestly, Dr. Tillstrom might as well have suggested removing my left nut.

Another bassist. *Shyeah*, right.

I thought of all the objections I could make to his parents: We were number two on the call sheet, we'd worked so hard . . . but none of them would make any difference. Especially not with Evan's dad.

And did I really need to convince them to let us play the PfefferFest? Evan needed surgery. He should have surgery. Period.

But there was more to it than that. I could see it in the way Ev's dad looked at labels of pill bottles while Evan cried, and how Mrs. Tillstrom, with the broken blood vessels in her eyes, stared emptily out the window, nothing left of her but her profile, which was all lines and arches.

There was something else about our reflections too. I could see myself most clearly, since the lights were on in the kitchen behind me. But the reflection seemed to divide itself while I watched, so that it seemed there were two Noahs—a dark outline and another more golden one that was a trick of the light over the stovetop.

Worse than that, there was no Ev in the reflection. I told myself it was because the back of the sofa was blocking it, but it didn't make any difference.

It was like Evan had disappeared.

The darkness that had snuffed the streetlights earlier tonight was eating him from the inside out.

"Evan," I said. "What do *you* want?"

"It's not about what he wants, Noah," Dr. Tillstrom said. "It's about what's best."

Mrs. Tillstrom shushed him. "I wanna hear this. Ev, honey, what *do* you want?"

And that was when I knew she was on our side.

Ev peeled his face away from the sofa. It was a red puffy mess, but at least it cast a reflection in the window. "I want to be a rock star."

Dr. Tillstrom stood to his full height. His jaw was clenched so tight I could practically hear him grinding the enamel off his teeth. "Evan. Son. You know that isn't a viable career path."

Ev turned away and looked out the window into the black night. "Yes, Dad. That's what *you* decided. *This* is what I really want. I want to be on a stage. I want to play bass. I want to sing backup. I want girls to dig me." He wiped his nose on the back of his hand. "That last part could be a problem."

Mrs. Tillstrom said, "Evan, honey, I've told you a million times: It won't be a problem for the right girl. Someone will recognize your good qualities and want to be with you no matter what. And they would be lucky to have you."

"The PfefferFest is tomorrow," I said. "I know somebody died there, but we've worked hard, and Evan's good. He's really good. Will a few more days really make a difference?"

Evan's dad sighed. His jaw relaxed. "Are you sure this is what you want?" he said to Ev. "Because you're playing chicken with your life. You know that."

"*Duh*, it's what I want. I've been trying to tell you for months."

Dr. Tillstrom found the pills he was looking for and shook some out into his fist. There were a lot of them.

"Here," he said to Evan. "They won't help in the long run, but they'll hold you through the weekend." He turned as if he were leaving, then slouched and turned around.

"You haven't been here, son," he said. It was an accusation. And Dr. Tillstrom never accused anyone of anything. "You've been out with Noah every night. I was hoping that we could at least have dinner together as a family."

"Why, Dad? So you can say nothing other than 'Pass the lasagna'?"

"No, Evan. I've stored up a lot of things I want to say." He took a deep breath. "I don't like your hair. I don't know why you damaged it in that way. I don't like your low scores on your SATs, because that's just laziness. I know you're smarter than that. I hate it that you stopped playing basketball, because I think you could've had a great college career before you became a doctor or a lawyer.

"But this thing with the PfefferBrau Haus? You're seeing it through to the end. And I'm proud of you for that. But then again, I would've been proud of you no matter what. I love you, Evan."

I saw the look in his eyes as he planted a wet smooch on Ev's forehead, and I knew, somehow, that that kiss was about more than just love. It was a blessing, and a letting go.

"All right. You've got until the PfefferFest. No more. Do you hear me?" he said, closing his medicine bag. "Then you agree to everything else. Not just the operation, but the treatments. Every single one. If they say to report to oncology twice a week, you're there twice a week, whether or not you're puking your guts out. Do I make myself understood?"

"PfefferFest," Ev agreed. "Then operation. Then puking. Got it." He leaned back in his pillow.

Mrs. Tillstrom got up from the recliner. "I take back all the rotten things I've ever thought about you, Noah," she said, pinching my cheek like I was two years old. "You're a good friend. Come on, Harald. Let's give these two some room. It's about time our son told Noah why he thinks it'll be so hard to get girls."

They left. I heard the hallway light click off and the bedroom door close gently, but I knew they weren't sleeping.

Evan closed his eyes. He wasn't crying anymore, but he wasn't talking either. Part of him must've hoped that I would go away and leave him in this glass house at the top of a hill where he could pretend, for just one more night, that the whole world lay at his feet.

But here was the problem: No way was I leaving.

I went into the kitchen, checked the cereal cupboard, and found the Smurfberry Crunch. I poured some nuggets into a salad bowl and put it on the coffee table.

Ev still didn't look at me. So I crunched down on a few neon-blue pellets. Nothing. I tried tempting him with a Fresca. I found a six-pack of them in the fridge and popped open two. I sat on the coffee table and gripped his hand as though he might drift off and it was up to me to anchor him there.

How could I not have felt it before? His hands were different from mine. They had calluses in different places. And now that I looked at him real close, I realized that a lot of things about Evan were different. The hair, for example. And underneath that, his damaged head that needed pieces scooped out, like a cantaloupe.

Now, see, this is what Mrs. Frizzell in senior English would call irony. I'd always thought Evan and I were the same. Once I admitted we were different people with different needs and wants, I mutated into a better friend.

"Noah," Ev whispered, and even though his voice was quiet, it was commanding.

I leaned forward.

"You know how you always say you'd give your left nut for something?"

I THOUGHT THE MARR HAD GOTTEN TO EV through his shark bite—that long diagonal scar along his rib cage.

It turns out I was wrong. He stood up and dropped trou.

Ev had no left nut.

It took me a while to figure out what I was supposed to be looking at. I mean, I didn't want to stare at his dick or anything. Then I understood what I was seeing. This wasn't about his dick—it was about his balls.

At first I wanted to heft his equipment and touch that emptiness. I held back.

"Jesus. Did your mom and dad have you fixed or something?"

"I knew you wouldn't understand."

He pulled his pants back up and collapsed on the sofa, turning his head away from me.

After what we'd been through together, how could he think I wouldn't understand? We both knew there was more to us than what you could see and what they called us in high school. This kid had helped me bury a deer—and that was only one item in the long playlist of our lives.

"Evan," I said. "Look at my face."

For a long time he didn't move. Then he turned over. "What."

I pointed to the scar on my nose. "I know what pain is," I said.

Ev snorted. "Not like this. You don't even know the meaning of the word "pain" until your testicle swells to the size of a cantaloupe."

"A cantaloupe? Seriously? How could I not have seen that?"

"You didn't look," he spat at me, and turned away again.

I deserved that.

Evan backed off. "It's not your fault, Noah. Nobody knew. I was real careful about it. I always went behind the shower curtains in the locker room to change. Then Mom saw me naked one day, freaked out and told Dad, who took a look and told me it was 'concerning.'"

"That's when you had your operation," I said, remembering. The one that was not an appendectomy but a ball-ectomy. I didn't even know what to call those. "You could've told me the truth."

He snorted. "No offense, man. I think of you like a brother and everything, but you're not exactly the most stable person in the world."

Something came up to me through the soles of my feet. I felt infected with courage.

"Ev," I said. "I'm here now, aren't I?"

He chewed on his lower lip, which was wobbling like a bowling pin. I thought he might bawl again, but he was cried out. For now.

"It's been so hard, Noah. First they told me I'd be sterile. They made me jerk off into a cup. They said they'd freeze the sperm and if I ever wanted children, they'd have to impregnate a girl with a turkey baster. And that's when I knew I wouldn't be going to the prom."

"But you hate the prom. You said it was uncool and a waste of money."

He shook his head. "It's not about the prom, Noah. It's about girls. Can you think of any of them who'd put up with this?" He grabbed at his equipment.

"Why? Does everything still work?"

"You mean can I still get it up? Yeah. That's what the doctors say. But honestly, the idea of any girl getting close enough for me to try freaks me boneless. And now they're going to open up my head. Bald and neutered. Like some ancient, smelly cocker spaniel."

Sonia had one of those. Evan was nothing like that idiot dog.

"It wasn't supposed to spread," he went on. "That's

what the doctors said. That's how I got my shark bite. They took a sample of lymph nodes and said I was clean, that I didn't need chemo. But they were wrong. It's metastasized. Now it's everywhere. The worst is in my head. So they have to take a buzz saw to my skull and scoop my brains out with a melon baller."

Ev was afraid. But Ziggy said that fear was the worst part of the Marr. Fear, I could help with.

"What rhymes with melon baller," I said.

"Taller," Ev suggested. He was starting to relax.

"Holler," I added.

"Even better."

I hummed the tune I'd been tinkering with earlier— the one that sounded like strength to me.

Scoop my brains with a melon baller
Make me scream
Make me holler
But you can't change who I am

I saw a ghost of a smile cross Evan's lips. "That's not bad, Noah," he said.

This time, when he turned away from me, I knew he wasn't gone. He was just resting.

For now.

I DIDN'T GO STRAIGHT HOME THAT NIGHT. I went back to north-west Portland and parked Ginny by the brewery.

Even after Ev told me what was really going on, and how tomorrow was his last chance to do what he wanted, it was more important than ever that I do everything I could to keep my friends safe.

I still didn't know exactly what the Marr was. I only knew what Ziggy told me. *Have to cut the Marr off at the source*, he said. *Have to do it with music*, he said. *Has to be you.*

I also knew Jurgen Pfeffer was a twisted sleazeball and he'd imported something evil and toxic from the dark forests of Germany, and we all knew what happened to kids in German tales when they went up against pure evil, didn't we?

• • •

I paced all four of the brewery blocks, looking for a way in to kill that evil thing so the music could go on but the poison would stop. No one else needed to disappear.

All around were garlands, graphics of hops, banners of guys in lederhosen clacking steins. Everywhere the cosmetic message: We're harmless. Come in and have a good time.

Little Pfeffer came and went, wearing giant rubber boots, his blond hair ruffled. That guy had bigger muscles since I'd last seen him. He was the size of a city block himself.

I shadowed him for a while, but he was careful to lock doors behind him. Tending his hardware, no doubt. I wondered if he knew what his brother was up to, or if he thought he was just crafting a really good beer.

When the sun came up that Saturday morning, I'd given up. The PfefferBrau Haus was locked down tight.

There was nothing I could do but play our set and hope Ziggy was right, that hitting it with the best set we could play would make the Marr slink back to the depths of the Bavarian forests from which it came.

All the same, a loop kept playing through my head: *Noah, awake! Who do you want to kill?*

By now it had become obvious to me that I wasn't the angel of the story.

I was the hit man.

• • •

There was no point going back to Gresham, so I let myself into the Maxi Pad, called Cilla and Idiot Willy, then opened the store as though it were any other day. Jojo was already up. "I'm too excited, man. You guys are gonna sound awesome."

Everyone else came in not long after in Jaime's car, too hyped to do anything but pound stuff. Ev didn't even grimace as Sonia gave the hi-hat an extra-loud *thwang* when Jojo and Crock loaded it into the van. Those pills Dr. Tillstrom gave Evan by the handful? They may not have been helping him long-term, but they seemed to keep the headaches down.

Before we knew it, it was 4:00 P.M. The PfefferFest had started at noon, but we weren't there. We were still at Jojo's, folding flyers for the girls to hand out downstairs.

I looked at my clock again. Cilla was still nowhere to be seen.

This was going to backfire on me big time. As number two on the call list, we were forbidden to arrive or unload until 6:00, which left Cilla only two hours, if she arrived now, to work her magic.

When Sonia wasn't drumming every surface with her thumbs, her leg was so twitchy it looked like she was having a seizure. I got dizzy watching her try to hold still. It was like looking at an earthquake.

So the Old Girls went downstairs to hand out flyers to the teenyboppers who came through ("Live! At the Pfef-ferBrau Haus! The Gallivanters explode the night!") and to take out their twitches on the glass cases of bumper stickers and rock buttons, ninety-five cents apiece. Jojo's Records was a big stop to and from the brewery. Jojo, with uncanny business sense, had preordered extra buttons that read "Totally Tubular" and "Gag Me with a Spoon."

Which left Ev and me upstairs, making up more goldenrod flyers. I don't know why the copy shop couldn't just call it yellow. Goldenrod had seemed like a good idea at the time, but honestly, now it looked like a tropical disease.

There was no sign of Ziggy yet, but I didn't think there would be. He never appeared until it was time to sing.

Crock shuttled back and forth to the brewery to keep an eye on how the other bands were doing. But he knew who I was really worried about. And it wasn't other bands, many of whom, Crock told us, hadn't figured out that "power ballad" was an oxymoron.

"They're so bad they're painful," he said. "There was this one singer in a mullet who kept barking 'Sheila' over and over again. That's it. He was trying to be all sincere, but he just looked constipated."

Crock had taken to perfuming himself these days, and he was sporting so much Polo for Men I didn't need a spoon to help me gag.

"Yeah yeah," I said. "What about Pfeffer?"

He shook his head. "I don't know what you're getting so worked up about, Noah," he said. "He hasn't gone anywhere. He stands at the entrance and squeezes the hands of pretty girls. Looking deep into their eyes. 'I'm so glad you came.' I may be sick." He made noises like he was hawking up a fur ball.

"Crock is right. Picking up girls doesn't make him a psychopath," Ev said. He, out of all of us, seemed least jittery. But then again, he was heavily medicated.

I couldn't help it: I did worry about Pfeffer. He was evil. I didn't want him anywhere near the Old Girls. I figured he would try to make a move on Sonia, because she looked like Tracy del Campo. And what was worse, she might fall for it. He was sophisticated. He knew how to say the right things. That was why I wanted to make sure someone was watching her every second we weren't onstage.

That was my plan: Have someone keep an eye on Sonia until we played our set, then play so well we'd explode the Marr into a million pieces, shove those pieces in a vat, and make Jurgen Pfeffer drink it, the sick fuck.

I chewed on an already bloody hangnail.

"Right. You know your assignment for tonight?" I asked Crock.

Crock huffed. "Goddamn, Noah. How many more times do we have to go through this?"

"Humor me."

He looked at his watch. "Shadow Sonia every second she's not onstage."

"And?"

"Keep her away from the sleazebucket. The one who makes me look like a monk."

"And?" Evan spoke up from where he was folding flyers.

Crock seemed flummoxed. That was as far as I'd coached him.

"And . . . don't drink the cannibal beer, no matter how good my ID is?"

Ev looked up. There was a sharpness in his eyes that hadn't been there a second ago.

"There are two Old Girls." His lips smushed themselves bloodless. He was about to blow.

"You're talking about Jaime, right?" Crock said. "Listen, as far as I'm concerned, while I'm on the clock I'm on Sonia duty 'cause we think she's the next target. But I'm happy to check on Jaime from time to time, especially if she's wearing that sweater that shows off her—"

Ev leaped up.

"Okay, time to go," I said, and pushed Crock out the door.

Ev grabbed the thing nearest to him, a bunch of goldenrod flyers, and threw them at the slammed door. Jaundice-colored paper rained down on the apartment.

As soon as it stopped raining flyers, I crouched down and started picking them up. They weren't very good. No graphics. We couldn't think of any logo to go with "galli-vanter."

Evan was still fuming. Over Jaime. At first I thought he was just mad at Crock, but then I remembered what had happened last night before I'd gotten Evan home and found out what was really at stake.

I sat cross-legged on the floor. "Listen, I'm sorry about what happened between me and Jaime in the store. It was stupid," I said, even though it hadn't felt stupid at the time. It had felt right. "The rule has always been hands off the Old Girls."

Evan started folding more flyers at Jojo's table. He didn't seem to be in a forgiving mood.

"But really. There's nothing to worry about. It's not like we planned it. It's just, when I came downstairs Jay was teary because her mom was going to pull the plug on us. She just needed a shoulder to cry on and I was there. It didn't mean anything. She knows it; I know it."

It was a small lie. It had meant something to me. Who knew how Jaime felt?

"Listen," I said. "If it'll make things any easier, I'll kiss you."

Evan slammed his hand on the table. "Goddamn it, Noah, do you have to make a joke out of everything? When you said 'No Old Girls,' you really meant Crock and I couldn't have them, but you could do whatever you want."

"That's not true. I swear. It was a spur-of-the-moment thing. It won't happen again."

"It'd better not," Ev said. He started folding the flyers again. All the rage seemed to seep out of him.

It was the maddest I'd ever seen him. And while I knew he had a lot going on, I couldn't help thinking: The Old Girl ban had been in place for years. Why hadn't he been this mad when I went out with Sonia?

A few minutes later, the door burst open and at last my sister came in, hauling a vinyl suitcase covered in flower decals behind her. She dumped it on the floor with a *thunk*.

"I'm here, nimrod. Where do you want me to set up?"

Cilla was wearing cutoff lace gloves, and her big hair was pulled off her face in a polka-dot doo-rag, like the *We Can Do It!* poster from World War II.

Jaime and Sonia followed, pulling a rolling rack of clothes that looked like it had come out of a Hollywood back lot. I saw feathers. I saw sequins.

I hoped they weren't for Ev and me.

Maybe asking my sister to be our stylist was a big mistake. But I didn't think so. The way I saw it, she got us hooked on the rock 'n' roll lifestyle by doing Evan's makeup to look like Bowie for that look-alike contest, which he won, which led us to Jojo, which led us to practicing more hours than we were awake.

My sister would come through for us again. She heaved the suitcase onto Jojo's dinette, flipped a couple of snaps, and up popped an armory of beauty products. She selected a pair of scissors and held them up for all to see.

Snickt snickt went her scissors. "Who's first?" She eyed Evan's dreads like they were cooties.

She started with me. She'd already cut my hair, so she focused on my wardrobe. She made me lose the dog collar. Then she geared me out in this shirt that buttoned down the side and accessorized it with a bandanna. It was very *Magnificent Seven*. I looked like a rebel: tough but not obnoxious.

But that was nothing compared to what she did with Ev.

She'd found him a set of leopard-skin pajamas and thrown a red velvet smoking jacket over the ensemble.

All of Evan's dreads encircled him on the floor. When they were on his head I hadn't noticed how disgusting they were. Now they were so filthy they seemed sinister, as though at any moment they might start inching back toward Ev to infect him with something else. Cilla swept them up, put them in the trash, and took the trash right out to the dumpster. Apparently I wasn't the only one who was grossed out.

And when Ev stood up, he looked free. His natural, baby-fine blond hair fell in waves around his head. You could really see the Swedish guy in him. He looked like Dr. Tillstrom, only younger, less hunched over, and with higher cheekbones.

He didn't look a thing like David Bowie.

He looked like himself.

He turned to me. I had to admit that Ev was a good-looking dude. The high cheekbones, the gentle blue eyes. But the best part? The best part wasn't just that he was handsome, but that he could feel it.

Angel, awake.

This was what he had wanted. This was why we put off his surgery. This was why I was putting us all in danger.

I didn't know how we would sound tonight, but it almost didn't matter. All Ev had to do was stand onstage and the girls would love him.

"Ev," I said. "It's good to see you, man. How do you feel?"

Ev smiled a lopsided grin at all of us that looked newly, surprisingly charming. "Ready," he said.

It was getting dark outside, but the coming night didn't freak me out. At this time of year, twilight could linger for hours.

We weren't finished yet.

23

THE CLOSER I GET TO WHAT COMES NEXT, the more I shut down.

First goes my eyesight. Things start to blur along the edges till everything—even the furniture—looks like ghosts. Then goes my hearing in a tinny hum, thanks to rock 'n' roll. Then all the feeling goes out of my body, beginning with my fingertips, and I feel cold—oh, so cold—and it's like I'm floating through space.

When this happens, I grab on to anything to anchor me. Most of the time the underside of a mattress. I scrunch my eyes tight, and wait to come back to earth.

The first thing I noticed about the PfefferBrau Haus that evening was that it was hot. The hops fug that covered the city was thick as Jell-O. Something was definitely brewing.

While Ev and I were waiting to get in, the world had

gotten fuzzy at the edges, the way it sometimes did when Ziggy was around. But Ziggy wasn't there, so I blamed it on the heat.

"Hey. How ya doin'," Ev said to about the twelfth girl who wouldn't stop staring at him.

"Remind me why we can't go straight in?" I asked him. "Isn't there a special entrance or something? Where the hell is Crock?"

Ev scoffed. "In the beer garden, probably. No big loss. And I thought we were waiting for the Old Girls, so we'd all go in together."

It was true. Cilla had shooed us out of the Maxi Pad after Ev's makeover. "Girl stuff," she said. "Go do a sound check or something." I was about to make a comment about Pfeffer's tight schedule and that it was only 5:00, but I thought better of it. Given a choice between facing down Mr. Psycho Eurotrash Brewmeister or my older sister, I chose Mr. Psycho Eurotrash Brewmeister.

So Ev and I decided to join the line that was snaking around the block, waiting to get in. Then when the girls showed, we'd cut the line. That was the plan.

Gradually, as we inched forward, I started to realize something: Kids were getting turned away. There were groups here and there, mostly boys but a few dumpy girls, who were walking away from the entrance, and they didn't look happy.

"This is so, like, totally bogus," I heard one girl say. Her shirt practically blinded me, all acid green and orange, so many belts hanging from her waist she looked like she had a hernia problem.

"Excuse me," Evan said, flashing her his new confident grin.

The girl stopped, got an eyeful of Evan, and cocked her hip. She was with a friend who was taller, with stringy brown hair and a mouthful of yellow, mossy teeth.

"What's going on up there?" Ev asked.

Acid Hernia Girl smacked her gum. "The old guy up ahead? The one with the accent? He says they're at capacity and can't fit anyone else in. He said something about losing their license. And we're majorly bummed. We came all the way from Troutdale for this."

"You here to see the Crazy 8s?" I said.

"Nah," the girl to her right said, and she pulled a familiar goldenrod piece of paper from her rhinestone-studded purse. My breath caught. Ev didn't look at me. We tried to pretend we'd never seen a flyer like this before. "These guys are like the house band at Jojo's Records. They're really good."

It wasn't every day you're shown your own press. I looked up at these two, who were ogling Evan. Only Evan. They didn't say anything like, *Hey, aren't you those guys? The Gallivanters?* They just thought Ev was a good-looking kid.

Evan scratched his downy chin and said, "Have you heard them before?"

"Oh yeah. Jojo plays their demo all the time," Mossy

Teeth said. "And then, like, sometimes we hear them through the ceiling of the store. They practice upstairs. The singer has this sexy voice. I think he's English or something. I bet he looks like Sting."

"Or David Bowie," Acid Hernia Girl said.

"And there was this one time they were rocking so hard this hunk of plaster came down from the ceiling and nailed this kid on the toe."

Evan coughed. "Was the kid's dad a lawyer?"

Acid Hernia Girl gave the fakest laugh I'd ever heard and play-slapped Evan on the arm, like, *Aren't you the cutest, wittiest thing?*

"It's okay," Mossy Teeth said. "He didn't feel anything. It landed on his Doc Martens. Thick soles."

I thought about explaining how soles were *under* the shoe, and what she was describing was the *upper* . . . Ah, forget it. Not worth the effort.

The girls looked at each other, then at Ev. "If they're turning everyone away, maybe you guys want to get pizza or something?"

Ev was done with them. "We'll take our chances on the line. Thanks, 'bye." And he turned away, looked straight at the wall—and even started flecking bits of beige paint from the hot bricks.

It wasn't anything I hadn't seen Ev do a thousand times before, but that was the old Ev with the clown hair. And those two trend-sucking mall rats from Troutdale? We didn't want them, but they'd been looking for someone to crush on. And Ev was it. The brush-off was funny when he looked goofy, but now that he was handsome, it was rude.

"You're going to have to work on your easy letdowns. You're a rock star now."

He trained his eyes on me. "I'm only a stud for tonight, remember? Then I turn into Frankenstein." He scratched his scalp, as if he were already feeling the staples holding his skull together.

He had a point.

I looked at my Mickey Mouse watch: 5:55. "This is bad," I said. "I think we should skip the line and go to the front."

Ev looked over my head in the direction of Jojo's. I craned around too, but didn't see any Old Girls. "Give 'em a few more minutes."

We didn't have a few more minutes. We had maybe two, and then Pfeffer would kick our asses out before we even got in. Evan wouldn't get his dream, the Marr would spread, and every child in the Northwest would wink out one by one.

I pulled him out of the line. "Come on, man. They're on their way. They'll make it. Ziggy too. We need to tell Pfeffer we're here."

Ev pulled me back. He had a strong grip for such a skinny guy. "What did you just say?"

"I said they'll show."

He frowned. "Exactly who are you expecting to show so we can play our set?"

"You know," I said. "Jaime. Sonia. Ziggy. Crock and Jojo are already inside."

He frowned and bit his lip.

"I need you to clear something up for me," he said. "You're worried about *Ziggy* not showing?"

"No," I said slowly. "I just said he'd be here, didn't I? And the girls will too." I looked at my watch again. "But right now we can't wait. Come on. It's time."

I grabbed Evan's arm and pulled him up the line, past a bunch of people who didn't mind flipping us off, around a corner, to where Jurgen Pfeffer was standing in front of the red velvet rope, wearing an expensive suit and a turtleneck underneath, even though it was a hot day. Not even a drop of sweat on his forehead, while everyone around him was brewing in the heavy air.

He was consulting something on a clipboard as a group of kids stood close by, waiting for him to notice them and let them through.

"Hi, Mr. Pfeffer. We're here," I said.

He didn't even look up from his clipboard, but put his arm firmly on the velvet rope at the entrance. "I'm afraid you'll have to take your place at the back of the line. As you can see, there's no more room inside until someone leaves."

"It's not like that. We're the Gallivanters."

That made him look up. "Oh, indeed." He squinted at me. "Yes, yes, I see," Pfeffer went on. "You've changed your hair since we met at Coffee Invasion."

"Got tired of looking like toxic waste."

His eyes shifted to his clipboard. He scratched his temple. "I've been meaning to get in touch with you. You see, the latest band is running a bit late and most of my customers are here to see the Crazy 8s. So I'm afraid I won't be able to offer you a spot in our lineup after all."

Did he just say what I thought he said? And so easily too? I wanted to bash that smug look off his face. How could he do this to us? We had to get in. We had to play. That was the bargain.

Ev tried to get him logically. "I don't understand. You said be here at 6:00. It's now 5:58. We did what you said."

Pfeffer looked at his own watch, which did not have Mickey Mouse on the face. The man had really hairy wrists.

"According to my German watch, it is now 6:03," he said, completely emotionless.

He was really going to do this to us? I hadn't prayed in years, but I prayed now. *Oh, Ziggy, where are you when we really need you? Just get us in. Face down this guy like you did before, and I'll carry us the rest of the way.*

Pfeffer was still talking. "It's just business. I'm sure you understand." He kept writing on his clipboard. He didn't look up. As far as he was concerned, we were already gone.

I got crazy-dizzy then, like I was going to black out, and leaned against a brick wall. No. I couldn't let this asshole win. There was too much at stake. There had to be another way. But I couldn't think of one.

Evan was the first to sense the change in the air. He craned his neck around, saw something he approved of, and turned back to Pfeffer, the corner of his mouth twitching like it was about to curl up. It was the smile he used to flash on the basketball court when he was about to fake someone out and drive the ball all the way to the basket.

He had Pfeffer. I didn't know how, but he had him.

"Sure," Evan said. "We understand. The girls will be disappointed, though."

I turned around. Slinking toward us were two girls who might once have been Sonia and Jaime.

Cilla trailed behind them, carrying a comb and with a bottle of hairspray clamped to her belt like a weapon.

Sonia's black hair was combed and combed again, plastered back from her head and secured with a little round leopard-skin cap. Everything else on Sonia was black and skintight—black jeans, zip-up jacket. She looked mysterious, like a Russian spy.

But that was nothing compared to Jaime.

Cilla had kitted her out in a skintight satin sundress with a slit up the leg that made her sway when she walked. Her lips were deep red, almost purple, and she kept them parted slightly. I don't know what Cilla did to straighten that crazy froofy perm, but now Jaime's hair looked downright silky, falling past her shoulders in shiny waves. And when she glanced to the side, I could see that Cilla had covered the shaved patch over her left ear with a gardenia, Billie Holiday style.

Sugar and spice, only with old-style movie glamour.

Cilla sauntered up to me and shot me a smile that looked a lot like Evan's slam-dunk grin.

"You're a friggin' genius," I said.

"About time you admitted it, nimrod. You just make sure everyone knows who your stylist is. I expect to get paying customers from this."

I don't know where she planned on putting these customers, since she didn't have salon space and hadn't even been to beauty school yet, but I would let her worry about that.

Meanwhile, the Old Girls slunk up to where we were talking to Pfeffer. Sonia lit a cigarette and blew smoke in a perfect ring from her Russian-spy lips.

Everyone stared. Men, women—I think even the brick walls looked, waiting to see what we'd do next. We hadn't played one lick, but already we were onstage.

"Sorry we took so long," Jay said, standing in a way that made her legs seem two stories tall. "I hope we're not too late."

Pfeffer took her hand in both of his and stroked it. "Not at all. I was just explaining to your bandmates what good sports the Crazy 8s are. Right this way, ladies," he said with a wolfish smile. He unhooked the velvet rope and ushered us into hell.

I'D NEVER BEEN INSIDE THE BREWERY BEFORE, so I suppose it shouldn't have surprised me that the four blocks of beige brick building surrounded a large open courtyard. Space enough for big trucks to back into. Ancient, unused rails were embedded in the asphalt under our feet. They were probably really handy one hundred years ago when the original owners of the brewery wanted to get their beer to the rest of the country chop-chop. Keep it mountain fresh, and all that.

Now the place was hung with hopvines wilting in the heat. People were packed in like cattle, and the smell of grilled gray sausages and onions filled the air. The only ones happy were the ones who actually got to drink beer in the roped-off beer garden. The underage crowd, which was the bulk of us, was crammed into the open-air mosh pit, but no one was moshing, thanks to the bland, piped-in, prerecorded, between-live-sets music. They all stared at a loading dock, which would be our stage.

Jojo and Crock started setting up our equipment. Jojo was assembling the drum kit. He worked efficiently, no trace of that hippie burnout lag.

Next to him, Crock strummed a chord or two on my guitar. Probably the only two he knew. He nodded and winked at the girls below.

Jurgen spared a glance at them. "I see your road crew is setting up, so you have a moment or two to spend with me." He leered first at Sonia, then at Jaime. "Come. Let us celebrate your debut." He put a hand on the smalls of their backs and steered them toward the one place in the crowded festival where people were actually having a good time.

I told myself I'd been expecting the leering, the mauling, that he'd be all over them like an octopus, but that didn't make seeing it any easier. I had to choke down a sick feeling in my throat, like I'd just been served a frosty mug of human remains.

The beer garden was cordoned off with another velvet rope, where Little Pfeffer sat in front, holding a tiny flashlight and croaking, "ID, please." No waders from the night before. He had on this pink polo shirt that strained over his shelflike man boobs. The pink shirt didn't make him look any wimpier. Pastels or no, he'd have no problem shot-putting a rowdy drunk.

Jurgen walked up to him, herding our girls, and said, "These two are with me."

Of course Little Pfeffer would look up. He looked up at everyone who tried to get past. But this look was a long one. We were standing right behind the girls, but as I mentioned, it was crowded, which might explain why I saw what he did next, but Evan didn't.

Little Pfeffer flexed his fingers and reached out. For what, I don't know. A handshake? A caress of skin and satin? It was subtle, then his hand and his gaze dropped back down to his lap. "*Ja,*" he said, but he might as well have said, *How come I never get the girls?*

Then he let them go through. Poor guy, with a brother like that who had actual moves and didn't mind flaunting his conquests. I couldn't help feeling sorry for him all over again, but not for long.

As soon as Cilla walked past and we tried to follow, his arm shot out and the red velvet rope came back up. "ID, please," he croaked.

"We're with them," Evan protested, pointing at the girls.

I pulled Ev away. As far as we were concerned, Little Pfeffer was made of marble.

Evan snarled at me. "Why'd you let him do that, man?" he said. "You promised they'd never be out of our sight. And we just let them walk away with that hound."

"Relax," I said. "Do you think I'd go into this without a Plan B?"

"Yes."

"And I don't blame you. But in this case you're wrong."

If I seemed smug to have done something right for once, can you blame me? But I'd get that smug smile beaten off my face soon enough.

Ev sniffed the air. I did too. That nasty beer fug that covered the city? It was now battling an even nastier fug from a cheap cigar.

Then I turned around and faced Idiot Willy. He was wearing a loud Hawaiian shirt and shorts that exposed legs that were way too white and hairy, but his face was all red. Probably from the heat. The hand that didn't prop up the stogie was wrapped around a frosty glass stein with "Coca-Cola" written in cursive on it.

He was here.

"Thanks for coming, sir."

I'd said "sir" a lot of times in my life, and sometimes to policemen, but I'd never meant it. I meant it now.

"Don't forget to call me Will, Noah. Is my idiot stepson doing his job?" he said.

It wasn't the first time in my life I wondered who the actual idiot in that family was.

Evan jerked his thumb behind him. "He's up onstage pretending to be Noah."

Willy looked to where he pointed. "I thought you told him to keep an eye on the girls?"

"We did," I said, and Willy smiled and puffed harder on his stinky cigar.

"I guess that doesn't surprise me," he said. "He never had any trouble watching girls. Just not the right ones. Speaking of which, where are Sonia and Jaime?"

"Beer garden," I said. "That asshole's got a paw on each of them."

Willy swore under his breath. "Already? That guy is a fast worker." He craned his neck around. "I don't see them."

"Yes, you do," Evan said.

Willy's eyes narrowed like a scope. He'd found them. "Lauren Bacall and Catwoman? Remind me how old they are?"

"Seventeen," I said. "My sister's work. She wants to be a beautician."

"Seventeen," he repeated, shaking his head.

"Officer," Evan said quietly. "They're still our girls."

"If you could find it in your heart, sir," I went on, and found the "sir" part came a little easier now, "we'd rather not bust them for drinking underage. We just want to make sure they're okay when we're not playing our set."

He took a sip of his Coke. "You don't have to remind me. I wouldn't want to see anyone's daughter getting groped by that guy. We've had our eyes on that particular individual for some time." He gestured to the beer garden where Pfeffer was smiling, hiding a mouthful of crooked teeth. "There's still a feeling you get . . . He seems to have zeroed in on Sonia."

I looked where he was nodding. Sure enough, Pfeffer

still had his arm on Sonia's back at the bar, but Jaime had shaken herself free. She carried a glass stein of something over to where Little Pfeffer was sitting. She put a hand on his shoulder and handed him the drink. I saw her say a few words to him and smile in a way that told me she might look like a movie star, but she was still Jaime, the one who trailed after everyone, picking up what needed picking up. In this case, an overlooked bouncer. Little Pfeffer said something back to her that may have been a simple thank-you, but I couldn't tell from this distance.

She patted him on the shoulder and dipped her head so her hair covered her face like a curtain. I couldn't read her expression. Then she left the beer garden and wandered off through an entrance that said TAPROOM over the door. Probably looking for the ladies'.

Which left just Sonia and her black cat suit to worry about. How did Cilla get her into that outfit, anyway? She must've had to lube up Sonia's skin really well. I put my hand to my nose and felt the texture of the scar she left me.

Yeah, she was gorgeous, and yeah, I'd always love her, but I'd never let her lead me around on a leash again.

Idiot Willy slammed the last of his Coke, leaving a residue on his droopy mustache. When he was done, he belched loudly and said, "Time to circle the wagons."

And in a gesture that you would never know was a signal, he wiped his mouth with the back of his arm.

In the beer garden, behind velvet ropes that were made of iron as far as Evan and I were concerned, at least four other guys with red faces and loud Hawaiian shirts nodded discreetly, as though they were paying careful attention to what their wives and dates were telling them.

Was it the red faces that gave them away as Portland's Finest? The mustaches? Or was it the fact that, even though they were sitting in the beer garden, they were all drinking Cokes?

With Jaime safely wriggled free and Sonia monitored by other, more qualified people, I turned my attention to our coming set.

Up on the loading dock stage, Jojo and Crock were almost done. We squeezed our way through the crowd to stand below them. "Thanks for keeping an eye on the girls, Crock," Ev said.

Crock crouched down to talk to us. "What? I'm doing my job. I can see fine from up here."

"Are they still in the beer garden?" Ev said.

"Sonia is," Crock said. "Is she wearing leather?"

Ev got real still. "Where's Jaime?"

Crocked scanned the crowds. "Is she wearing leather too?"

"Asshole," Ev muttered. "Where is she?"

"Relax," I said. "She's just in the bathroom or something. I saw her leave."

Evan got really still. I'd seen him like that before. Not often, but enough to know that he thought I'd done something really stupid and he didn't want to tell me straight. "How long ago?"

I looked at my watch: 6:20. She'd been gone only fifteen minutes. Plus she was a girl, so she might be putting on more lipstick or checking her hemline or something, but still . . .

My vision got blurry around the edges. And when I turned to my right, Ziggy was standing at my shoulder, looking feathered from head to toe. "Something's wrong," he said.

"I know. I can feel it."

"What, Noah? What can you feel?" Evan said, his words tumbling out like dice.

I looked out over the crowd. In the beer garden, Sonia was still blowing smoke around Big Pfeffer.

I zeroed in on Little Pfeffer sitting at his bouncing post. When had he changed his shirt? This one was inky black.

Then he turned to one side. His face was tattooed. This wasn't Little Pfeffer at all. It was some other musclehead who was just as wide but not as preppy.

A cold panic settled over me. Where had Little Pfeffer gone? And what had ever made me think he was harmless? The pink shirts? The fact that he didn't act like a hound? He was strong enough to knock a girl around and feel sorry about it later. Dad used to do that all the time.

Evan and I had spent a lifetime reading each other's cues. Any blood that might have been left in his face drained from it now. He was pale as marble. "Oh god," he said. "The bodybuilder?"

"Maybe it's nothing. Maybe I'm being paranoid."

Jojo didn't think so. He was crouched next to Crock on the loading dock. He didn't tell us to mellow out or offer us a spliff. "Get the fuzz, Noah. Get the fuzz now."

"I can't. They're in the beer garden and we can't get past—"

"I'm on it. You guys check the little girls' room," Jojo said, jumping down from the loading dock and picking his way through the crowd.

Crock cocked his head at the entrance behind the loading dock. "I always wondered what their bathroom looked like," he said, and he zoomed off. Why did he have to make everything sound so sleazy?

Then it was down to Evan and Ziggy and me.

"She won't be in the bathroom," Ziggy said.

"I know," I said.

"What?" Ev said. "You know what?"

"That she won't be in the bathroom."

Evan kicked the stage. "Fuck! I knew it. Where will she be?"

I didn't need Ziggy to tell me. "The hot room. He always

takes them to the hot room." By now I understood that "he" was not who we thought he was. We could see Big Pfeffer just fine from where we were. I now understood he was like Crock—skanky, but not dangerous.

Ev looked around at the warehouse entrances. There were lots of them. Four city blocks. That's how big this place was. Where would we even start?

"Great. How do we find *that*? This place is a maze. It could be anywhere. Goddamn, Noah, she's not like us," he said, tugging on his baby-fine hair. "She's got the wrong shoes for kicking ass."

"Shut up, okay? Just shut up."

I took a deep breath and closed my eyes, because I knew I would never get to the right place by looking for it. Not in time. It was something I'd have to feel. Or hear.

And then Ziggy whispered in my ear, "You could use a guide right now, son." And I knew he wasn't talking about himself.

My eyes snapped open. I shoved through the crowds to the front entrance.

"Noah! Come back! You're going the wrong way!" Evan said.

"Trust me," I said, and I ran out the front.

We sprinted down the street past the long line of people waiting to get in, Evan keeping pace with me. Ziggy was right with us. I didn't see him but I could feel his hair brush the back of my neck.

Ev looked up at all the brewery accessories—the

smokestacks, the water towers, the fire escapes. "Shit. What do you expect us to do? Follow the smell?"

"No. I got a better plan," I said, ogling the piles of trash that had blown against the buildings, looking for something shiny.

Evan huffed. "Will you at least tell me what we're looking for?"

"The guy with the tinfoil brain," I said.

We found Terrence in the spot where we'd first passed him that one night when Evan couldn't hide his headaches anymore.

He hadn't been there earlier, but I was glad he was there now. He was crumpled into a pile of rags. He had a new tinfoil crown.

I kicked him on the foot. "Wake up, soldier."

In less than two seconds, Terrence went from being asleep to being on his feet and saluting me.

"No time to spare," I said. "He's got her."

Terrence's eyes? The rheumy yellow ones? They cleared right up. "This way, sir," he said, and sprinted down the block in duct-taped shoes.

I would've missed the entrance completely if it weren't for Terrence. It was down a narrow alley, covered in shadow—and that beer fug? It was extra intense here. Evan coughed and wheezed but refused to slow down. I brought my kerchief up around my nose, hoping the cotton filter would help me catch my breath.

We followed Terrence into the alley and down a set of stairs that had a DANGER! HIGH VOLTAGE! sign on the railing.

We weren't fooled. There was no voltage.

We bolted down the stairs. At the bottom was an ancient door with one window and an iron grille over it, like you'd find in a mental institution.

Terrence fiddled with the door handle, which was so loose it rattled and heaved, but didn't give completely. Then he put his shoulder to the whole door and it caved inward. He stumbled in and we piled after.

We found ourselves in a forest of vats, each at least twenty feet tall. They were all cooking something, making a staticky humming noise while belching that intense hops smoke through the curled tubing that ran from the top of each. Too salty. Oh god. There was too much tang in the smell. I prayed that Little Pfeffer hadn't had time to add an extra ingredient.

How were we ever going to find her in this? There were at least twenty vats, all of them two stories high, the hatches on top reachable only by rolling staircases that had been shoved out of the way against the brewery walls.

She could be anywhere.

Evan pushed past us. "Jaime!" he called.

I heard a shriek that could've come from anywhere. It was a room of buzzes and echoes.

"Jaime!" he shouted again. I heard a metallic *bang!* Like someone had kicked the side of one of these giant vats.

Ev ran ahead and I followed. I lost track of Terrence.

Thank god for Ziggy. I'd forgotten he was with us. "Look, m'boy." He pointed at something lying on the ground. It was a wilted gardenia. The one Jaime had been wearing in her hair.

I grabbed Evan by the jacket and showed him what we'd found. "This way," and we wove off beyond the flower, calling her name. "Jaime! Jaime!"

And then came the sound we didn't want to hear. There was a splash.

It seemed like we rounded a corner and there he was, on top of a rolling staircase, his huge arms pinning something down into the metal vat. Jaime's head?

Little Pfeffer was broader than Ev and me put together. No way we could climb that thing and wrestle him down in time to save Jaime's life, if she was still alive in there. But she was. I could see those long fingers slapping and pulling.

Ev was smart. He went to the bottom of the rolling staircase, lifted knobs that locked the wheels in place, and kicked with everything he had.

The staircase tipped up. It seemed to hang there, balanced for an impossibly long time, then toppled over backward with a loud clatter. Pfeffer went down with it, falling twenty feet. He managed to twist himself in midair, and he landed on his hands and knees with a loud *crack!*

He looked up at me with loathing in his eyes. He leaned back on his heels and brought his hands off the floor, trying to rotate them. He said, without a trace of a German accent but with a profound stutter, "You b-b-b-broke my wrist, you little p-p-p-punk."

Why he said this to me and not Evan, I don't know, but I was ready for him. I ran at him while he was still down and, with one heavy boot, kicked him between the legs. He was an asshole. He was my dad. I had to protect my family from him.

"Steady on, lad," Ziggy whispered. "Help Evan first."

Ev was putting the staircase right side up. It didn't seem heavy, but it was large, with a platform at the top. He didn't even lock the wheels before he bolted up the steps and plunged his arm into the hatch. I saw him make a face. How hot was the liquid in there? Was Jaime already boiled alive?

I got beneath the ladder to hold it steady. I kicked the stops into place.

"Have you got her?" I called up. Nothing.

From below, I watched as Evan grabbed something long and red. Jaime's arm? *Come on come on heave!* I willed him. With a giant grunt he pulled, and she came out onto his lap. Her skin was red as a lobster's. Everything about her was slack and unmoving.

"Is she breathing?" I called up, and then I was slammed forward. My head hit concrete.

I rolled over to see what had hit me. Blood was dripping from my forehead into my eyes, but I could still make out Little Pfeffer standing over me. "You g-g-got no right," he said. "She was m-m-mine."

He was nursing his twisted wrist. He probably couldn't throw a punch. He didn't need to. He was like me. He was a kicker. He got a running start and slammed a penny loafer on the side of my head. And he kept slamming—my nuts, my ribs, my kidneys, my ears. I tried to kick back, to make him go over, but nothing seemed to stop him.

I curled myself into a ball, willing him to stop. But the kicks kept coming and coming.

Snickt!

The pounding let up.

I dared to uncurl myself. Little Pfeffer was still standing above me, but a glazed look had come over his eyes. His hand was at his throat as though he were the one drowning. Then came the blood. At first just a trickle under his left ear. Then there was a waterfall of it coming from all around his neck.

He fell forward, right onto me.

I kicked and pushed and finally managed to get him off. Above me, Terrence wiped his hunting knife on his filthy pants. He offered me a hand. "You all right, son?" he said, dusting me off. "You probably cracked a rib or two."

I wiped blood from my eyes. "Jaime?" I asked.

Terrence glanced up at the rolling stairs.

I knew Jaime was alive because she was shaking. Evan had her face pressed against his velvet jacket. "Don't look," he said to her, staring down at us in horror and relief. Then he started humming a soft lullaby to her, the way Cilla used to do to me when things got to be too much.

"That boy up there," Terrence said. "He's not bad in a fight." Then he spat heroically. Right on Little Pfeffer's face.

I heard voices in the distance, but I couldn't make out where they were coming from.

I looked down at the spreading pool of blood at my feet. Little Pfeffer wasn't getting up. He couldn't hurt any more girls.

Poor Terrence. What was going to happen to him? He'd saved all our lives.

I looked to Ziggy to say something, but he was blurry around the edges. And no wonder—when I brought my hand up to my right eye, I found it puffing up like a golf ball.

But I could still see the monster at my feet. "I don't know how this is going to go for you, Terrence. If you like, I can say I did it." And I meant it. It wouldn't be the first time I'd been in this kind of trouble.

"Don't be an idiot, boy. You got your whole life in front of you. Me?" He scratched his head using the handle of his hunting knife. His tinfoil crown slid over just a bit, exposing the skin covering the gray jelly of his damaged brain. Only, now I wondered how damaged it really was. "I don't do so well on the outside."

I heard voices calling my name.

"Over here!" I called back. I knew this place was a maze. I knew I should get Willy. But I couldn't take my eyes off Evan and Jaime, two stories above, and yet so far away they were in a story of their own. One that didn't include me.

But had I wanted to be the star of this particular show? Had I wanted to be the hero of her life? Did I want to be the one pressing her, grateful and trembling, against me while I hushed her down with lullabies?

It was only now, when I saw them together, that I realized the answer was yes.

Too late.

Ziggy came into focus. He was standing by my side. I realized he'd always been there. I felt something feathery brush my hair, and it was like a blessing. "Do you see now, lad?"

I could only nod. Because I did see.

I saw the way Evan smiled when he held her close and whispered in her ear. There would be no *thanks, 'bye* for this girl.

I understood what I should've known since the seventh grade with that stupid game of Mafia when he told me later that I should've killed Jaime *last*: She had always been the one Evan wanted. And then he'd gotten sick, and too scared to make a move.

I didn't know how long he'd been holding back this little tidbit from me, or why. Maybe he didn't know if I'd approve.

I like to think that since he'd told me about his operation, he would've eventually told me about Jaime, but now he didn't have to. I could see for myself, I could hear it in the way he hummed.

I listened to my breath whistle in and out and watched them through unreliable eyes.

More than anything, I understood that, much as I might have wished differently, this was the only way it could be—Ev was the one to save her, and I was the one left down here in a spreading pool of blood.

After all: He's the angel of the story.

And me? I'm the one who did what needed to be done.

I heard Willy calling again. Closer this time.

"Over here!" I called back.

There were more footsteps. Lots of them. Then Willy grabbed me by the arms, and, no matter how disgusting I was, all busted up and covered in blood, he hugged me like I was his own child. It hurt, but I didn't mind. I didn't want him to let me go.

But he did, and stood back. "Oh god. Not again, Noah. What happened to you? Are you all right? Where's Jaime?" He didn't need my help on that one. He heard the sobs, and soft humming, and looked up.

He tugged on his mustache, and as he pulled his hand away from his face, years of worry seemed to come away with it. I didn't care what Crock said: Willy was an okay guy. A defender of people who needed defending.

"And the suspect?" he asked.

I closed my eyes and took a deep breath. I lifted my arm, as though it was what I'd been put on this planet to do, and I pointed.

"HE DIDN'T HAVE AN ACCENT," JAIME SAID in the PfefferBrau break room a little later. The place was crackling with activity. Or maybe it was just static from the walkie-talkies of a dozen police officers who came in and out and took a lot of statements. Medics came and put blankets over us, but Jaime was the only one who needed one. When Ev had fished her out she'd been red all over, like she'd been boiled. But gradually her color was fading back to normal, even if her smell wasn't.

A cool shower and fresh clothes could fix that.

The rest of us got blankets and Cheez Doodles and foam cups of coffee, plus a steak for my puffed-up eye. Too bad I couldn't put a steak on my ribs too, and draw out the breakages.

Yeah. I thought I'd been worked over before, but that was nothing compared to getting my ass kicked by a

250-pound psycho bodybuilder. He'd been dead for an hour and I still felt shock waves, like he was slamming me against the floor over and over again.

Jaime went on: "I handed Pfeffer a Coke and he said, 'Thank you.' Didn't sound German at all. I suppose it could've meant a lot of things. I don't know why it creeped me out, but it did. I told him I had to go to the bathroom, mostly so I could get away without offending him. Can you believe it? I still thought the worst thing he could do was kick us out."

Jay was sitting in an elaborate oak chair that might've been a throne. Lions were carved into the armrests. Ev's velvet jacket was draped around her shoulders, and Ev himself was draped around that. He couldn't seem to stop touching her. He was acting like it was painful for there to be even an inch of space between them. And Jaime kept looking up at him, like she couldn't believe that Evan had such a profile, and that he was smiling a lopsided, soft smile at her.

Willy was taking notes on a flip pad. "And then what happened?"

"I'm not really sure, it was so sudden. One second I was looking for the bathroom, and the next he jumped me." Her lower lip started to wobble. "I tried to scream but he covered my mouth and told me that I couldn't just hand him a Coke like that and then walk away, that I was a tease and that it wasn't his fault."

"What wasn't his fault?" Sonia said.

"Killing me, I guess." She took a deep breath and leaned in closer to Ev. "He even tried to shut me up by singing a lullaby. He was a horrible singer. I kept thinking Noah would've had a cow."

I smiled. Bad idea. I almost spat out *another* molar.

Bad singer. Not German. Who knew?

Although, now that I looked around, the clues were there. The break room was decorated with posters of guys in lederhosen drinking foamy beer from giant steins; snowy Alps; and a white, princessy castle standing on a forested hilltop. The vending machines stocked Toblerone and Lindt chocolate.

They were trying too hard to be German—Jurgen with his Eurotrash suits, Arnie with his blond flattop—and the whole city had bought it. How pathetic were we?

Over the next few weeks, we'd learn from newspapers and TV that Jurgen and Arnie were actually George and Alf Cross. When Alf's charming little party trick of making teenage girls disappear threatened to catch up to them in their hometown of Cleveland, George suggested not only that they move here to the end of the map (where, among other things, there was more wilderness to bury bodies), but that they reinvent themselves.

Look at us. We're both blond. We could be German. What do German guys do? They drink a lot of beer. I know—we'll buy a brewery! It's brilliant!

I was disgusted with all of us. Except Evan and Jaime. And Willy. And Terrence, who had blood on his hands so I wouldn't have any on mine. I closed my good eye. I didn't know where he was now, but I hoped that, wherever it was, he was getting the medical attention he needed and deserved.

Now there was a scuffle outside the break room door.

"Let me through, man! I need to see the kids!"

I heard a female officer say, "Are you immediate family?"

"Hell, yeah. I'm their roadie."

The break room door opened a crack and then closed again without anyone coming through. Our police guard must've realized that "roadie" wasn't mother or father. "I'm sorry, sir, I'm going to have to ask you to leave."

I heard Jojo yell. He actually raised his voice. "Don't patronize me, lady . . ."

"Sir—"

"I once spent three days covered in mud at Woodstock so I could haul around amps for the Who."

"Sir—"

"I smoked reefer with John Lennon . . ."

"Sir—"

"And did coke with David Bowie in the back room of Max's Kansas City."

"Sir, if you're not a parent or legal guardian, you can't . . . Wait, you've met Bowie?"

Jojo's voice quieted. "Yeah. Way back when he was still gay. Or at least he thought he was. But he wasn't gay with me. At least, I don't think so. I'm pretty sure I'd remember something like that . . ."

Willy cracked open the door. "It's all right, DeeDee. Let him in."

Jojo came swaggering through and took in the scene— me sitting on one table, trying not to look pulped, and Evan draped around Jaime like a blanket.

"Evan! Dude!" Jojo said. "You finally made your move! That is so awesome. Whoa, Noah. Do you realize you're wearing eight ounces of chuck?"

I took the steak off my eye.

Jojo turned to Willy, still wearing his Hawaiian shirt but now with a badge hanging over his belt. "I thought you said they were all right."

"They are," Willy said. "Noah here took the biggest pounding."

"It's okay. I've had the most practice getting knocked around."

"Don't think that, dude. Don't ever think that. No one ever deserves to get busted up the way you did. Hey, are those Cheez Doodles?"

I handed him the bag I didn't even realize I was holding and put the steak back over my eye.

He took it and hopped up next to me on the octagonal lunch table.

Willy flicked his notepad shut. "I think that's all we need for now. Let's get Jaime home and cleaned up."

Jaime spoke so softly, I almost didn't hear her.

"Come again, hon?" Willy said.

"I said, I wanna play our set. We've been practicing for months. I feel like, if we don't play tonight, those two psychos win. And I don't want them to win."

"Jay. Sweetie," Jojo said, his mouth outlined in neon-orange dust. "You're breathing. They've already lost."

Evan added, "You don't have to do this, you know. You've been through a lot. There'll be other gigs." He wouldn't look at me, as if in not looking at me, he could make me shut up about the fact that there wouldn't be other gigs. Which meant that, however much he wanted to be a rock star, he wanted Jaime more. And again I wondered how I could've missed it. All that longing—it should have made him as raw as this piece of beef covering my right eye. And it probably did.

I must've been in a world of my own.

Jaime went on: "Look, I know what I'm asking. If I go home now, I'm a survivor. Just me. But if we play, then all of us are something more. I'm asking you. Please don't make the one image I see before I go to sleep tonight be that sicko with his throat cut."

And that was when Evan kissed her. I mean really kissed her, like if he tried, he could scour her brain with his tongue.

The room was filled with static and feet shuffling and other sounds of people trying not to look.

Jojo nudged me. "Cheez Doodle?"

Willy cleared his throat loudly to make Evan break

away. "I wish I could help you. I really do. But we've got to close this place down. It's going to take forensics months to go over everything as it is. They tend to frown on having hordes of kids trampling evidence. They're funny that way."

Jojo hopped down from the table. "No prob. I got this one. Come on, Noah. Leave the steak here."

I slapped the raw meat down on the table and followed him out, going slowly because with every step I felt like I was being skewered by my own ribs. At some point I'd have to get Dr. Tillstrom to fix me up. Again. Something told me that he wouldn't mind. With the Pfeffer brothers out of the way, our gallivanting days were almost over.

But not quite.

The break room must've been soundproof, because as soon as I stepped out, I heard a dull roar. I looked at the pipes running along the ceiling. What kind of brew made that noise? It got louder as we wove down a bunch of corridors, left and left and left again. I felt like some kind of Greek hero, who slew the monster and now had to get out of the labyrinth.

We climbed up a half set of stairs that were camouflaged by a pile of kegs, emerging behind the loading dock stage that opened onto the courtyard.

The roar hadn't come from the brew—it had come from the crowd. The whole courtyard was a mosh pit of kids, slamming each other forward, ready to start a riot.

Deputy Chief Simmons was there, decked out in gold gewgaws. He was standing in front of the mic, urging calm. I wondered how he could possibly think he could control a riot of teenagers when he was wearing something that was obviously polyester.

"I can't comment on an ongoing investigation. I'm going to have to ask you all to disperse and go home."

It didn't work. Kids hurled questions at him, and someone even pitched a gray sausage onto the dock.

Jojo had his arms tucked into his armpits. "The guy's got no idea what makes a good intro," he said, and strode out onto the stage, his arms lifted high in a victory sign. And even though nobody probably knew who he was, they all cheered him anyway.

Jojo grabbed the mic away from Deputy Chief Simmons and tapped it.

"This thing on?" A hush settled over everyone. I felt like the whole city was waiting. "Who wants to hear some rock 'n' roll?" I thought the roar of the crowd had been loud before. But when they yelled now, you could hear it in outer space. "Well, all right, then! Party at Jojo's Records!"

THE SIGHT OF JOJO'S BACK, TRIUMPHANT, whipping up the crowds to a celebratory frenzy—that's a memory I love.

There are other memories I keep of that year, but I don't treasure them as much. I don't even really like them, but I guard them anyway. Even if, by some miracle, someone came up to me and said, "I can take them from you, just for a while, so you can rest," I wouldn't give them up, because I don't trust anyone other than me not to forget.

And so I scrub them down and polish them up at night after the lights go out so I can keep them fresh.

To begin with, there's my first sight of Evan's bald skull and the line of black sutures, like ants, all around it. Or the look on Jaime's face when the surgeon told us he couldn't get all the tumors from Evan's head and urged us to get a second opinion.

Or the club gig in August, at Luis La Bamba, when

Ev, bald and bewigged, had to play sitting in a camp chair because chemo had made him too weak even to stand up.

And then there was that little scene in Emanuel Hospital over Labor Day weekend, when Jaime told Ev she wasn't going to go to her swanky New England college after all. He was so mad he threw everything he could at her. Lemon Jell-O. A vase of tulips. A bedpan, thankfully empty.

Or how, right after Jaime and Evan's colossal bedpan-flinging fight, I found Jaime in the hospital courtyard, sitting next to a planter of wilted purple flowers. She was all hunched over and racked with sobs, and she looked at me with snot running all over her face and told me she didn't blow off college completely, that she'd just deferred until January. "Mom says any longer and she'll lose the security deposit. She says we have to be practical. She asked me if I thought Evan would linger longer than that, and I said no. Can you believe it? I sped up his death for five hundred bucks."

I told her it wasn't her fault, and that Ev appreciated her sticking around even though he didn't show it. I told her that it had been her mom's idea to defer, so she had nothing to blame herself for. But I know what really wrecked her, which was that there was no going back. We'd put a timeline on Evan's life—something even the doctors wouldn't do, and that from now on it would take some serious stagecraft to make Ev think we still believed that anything was possible.

Or how about this for a charming little gem: When I woke up from my nap that October day in hospice and realized that Evan had reached the end, I could've nudged the rest of the family awake too. That's what I should have done. But I didn't. Because all I could think was, *What's going to happen to me without him?*

I'm not proud of hoarding his last moment, even though Mrs. Tillstrom still says she was glad it was me, because I was stronger than the rest of them, and I knew exactly how to ease her baby from this world. She never stops reassuring me that I did exactly what was right for Evan, but I know the truth, which is that I did exactly what was right for me.

And here we go. The last day, nothing omitted: Ev had been moved to a hospice on the west side of town, by the private school and the cemetery. But he didn't pay much attention to the view outside his window by then, and at least the inside of the place didn't smell like rot and Lysol.

I woke up from a catnap (Dr. and Mrs. Tillstrom and Jaime were still zonked out on couches around the room), listened to Evan's breaths over the clicks and beeps of the monitors, and realized they were slowing down. There were whole bars and measures between each one. At that pace, did a heart still even have a backbeat?

I acted quickly, before my conscious mind could kick in and convince me that nothing had changed. I lifted Ev's blankets and crawled into bed next to him. There was nothing left but a pile of kindling by then. I remember whispering, "Nothing to be afraid of, Ev. It's not death. It's only an echo." And I was humming, running my fingers over his bald head, when I heard a sigh. When I opened my eyes, I was left clutching a cold body. Dr. and Mrs. Tillstrom and Jaime were standing around the bed, dry-eyed but choking, clutching any bit of exposed skin on Evan's body, helping him leave us without worrying about what he'd left behind.

I carry these memories because it's my job. But Jaime had it right, sitting in the employee break room in the PfefferBrau Haus, after we saved her from being cooked into pale ale. If I let these memories overwhelm me, then I become a survivor and nothing more. And Evan was too important to be remembered as a heap of bones.

Let me leave you with a memory I'm happy to carry because we all created it. All that gallivanting? Looking for answers in record bins and coffeehouses? This is what it led up to. So picture this instead.

Jojo quickly realized that the store wasn't going to be big enough to hold everyone, so the two cops in the city who weren't at the PfefferBrau Haus cordoned off the streets in the blocks around Jojo's and let the whole city mill around. When I asked where our stage was gonna be, Jojo said, "No worries, man. Crock's running extension cords to the roof. The whole city can see you up there."

We listened as they clunked heavy equipment up the back stairs, while we primped in the Maxi Pad. Actually, Cilla primped Jaime. She even found a new slinky satin dress that didn't smell like a brewery. I have no idea where she got it, although I wouldn't be surprised if every boutique in the city had opened its doors for her if someone told them who it was for. Nobody knew Jaime's name yet, but everyone in the city knew there was finally a girl who got away.

Jojo came into the Maxi Pad and said, "It's time."

We followed him up the stairs and onto the roof.

When we walked out onto the tarry blacktop, we saw that Crock and Jojo had not only moved our amps and instruments up there, they'd also found multicolored footlights that were angled right where we were supposed to stand.

Sonia plunked herself behind her kit and played a rim shot. Three stories below, the crowd roared and pointed.

Sonia and Evan started our opening riff. A backbeat to Jojo saying, "Ladies and gentlemen, the reason you're all here tonight. The crew that caught a killer . . . Put your hands together for . . . the Gallivanters!"

Only then did I realize that Ziggy wasn't with us, and that I hadn't seen him since the hot room, and without him, we didn't have a voice. I was still worrying a loose molar with my tongue, and trying not to move too much so I wouldn't puncture a lung. Plus, as Jojo pointed out, my face looked like an eggplant. I was too damaged to front us.

Ev kept playing the opening riff and staring at me, waiting for me to jump in. He was starting to lose confidence.

I stepped up to the mic, ready to sing without Ziggy, when I felt something feathery brush my right shoulder.

It was always the right.

He put his hand over the mic before I could open my mouth. "No worries, lad. I'll take it from here."

I stepped back into the shadows and let Ziggy take over. But even Ziggy, with his suave voice and colossal presence, was nothing standing next to Evan.

I looked three stories below to the throngs that were packing the street. All those bright new-wave colors. Neon aqua. Neon pink. Neon orange. It was like looking at a field of stars.

When Ziggy opened his mouth to sing, I swear I could hear a softer, more subtle sound come from somewhere out there. It was the faintest of pops, like a bubble in a champagne glass. Then a sigh. And I knew that, somehow, one of the Disappearing Girls (or at least pieces of one) had reappeared, and that a family could try to breathe again. A tiny piece of darkness had been lifted.

With each pop, Ev seemed to stand straighter, his lopsided smile growing bigger and bigger. When he thought no one was looking (which in truth was exactly never), he turned his smile on Jaime, who was dancing behind the keys, looking as glamorous as a classic movie star.

All these months, people had been asking me why it had to be the PfefferFest, why we couldn't get a gig somewhere else. And I never knew what to tell them, because I didn't really understand it myself.

Looking at Evan's smile, I finally did.

He was why it had to be the PfefferFest. Not for the Disappearing Girls. He wanted to be a rock star. Now I realized something I'd only half understood for months— that *rock star* wasn't enough. It would be better if he were a hero too. I wanted him to mean as much to everyone in the world as he did to me.

I told myself I hadn't known that it would be Jaime that he'd save—only that he'd save someone, the way he'd saved me every day for years and years of my life.

I looked at him shine now, full of confidence and talent. He was brighter than the footlights, brighter than any wave—new or old. The man was practically a constellation all on his own.

And now he could get the credit he deserved, on this rooftop with the night sky above us and what looked like another night sky at our feet.

I sniffed the air.

No hops.

The darkness was ours again. At least for one night, we'd taken it back.

IT'S THE SUMMER OF 1985 NOW, the year *after* some science fiction writer said we'd all be under mind control and lose the ability to love.

I say: *Bullshit.* I've got plenty of love. Evan died last October, but he's still with me. Whenever I remember him, it's the way he was the night he fished Jaime out of the vat. Tall. Sharp profile. Heroic. In my memories he's always that way—not the clown-haired sidekick he really was for the last few years of his life.

I ask my therapist about this, about why my memory's so faulty where Ev's concerned, and he (my therapist) says not to be so hard on myself. He says I remember Evan as a handsome, talented guy because, to me, that was what he was always like.

"Remember what you told me about that game of Mafia? You've always thought of him as your better half."

We talk a lot about halves and wholes in his office. Especially when he tries to explain how my brain works. I'm not sure how much psycho talk I believe. All I know is this: Evan is gone, and I miss him. Most days, I know I'll never stop missing him.

I still work for Jojo. I rent the apartment on the floor above the Maxi Pad. It's really cold and used to be infested by rats, but I've cleared out the worst of those, thank god. Jojo and I have a "family" dinner most nights, and whatever we eat is okay by him. Whatever rent I pay is okay by him. Whatever I wear is okay by him, however many hours I work in the store are okay by him . . . you get the idea.

Jojo tells me stories about all the people he's loved who have gone, then he offers me another slice of pizza. I can practically hear him thinking: It's only a matter of time before *I* board a bus like the assistants of his past, and he's going to hold on to me for as long as he can. I am more than his assistant, but he doesn't know what else to call me.

I do.

When he gets all blurry eyed and talks about me going away, and how he'll be okay with that, really, I know what I have to do. I pat his hand and tell him that, even if I leave him, I will never really leave him. I tell him that, even though I've shopped around, I know for sure he's the best father I've ever had. And that seems to satisfy us both.

• • •

I still play guitar, do occasional session work, but I don't write songs anymore. It's not the same as it used to be. Jojo says I've lost my voice. I picture Ziggy glimmering off down the stairs when the music ended. Jojo doesn't know how right he is.

So most days you can find me right here, minding the store, smelling like glass cleaner because I'm always polishing something.

Which is in fact what I'm doing when a soft voice calls, "Noah." But underlying my name, a divine counterpoint to the tune, are the words *Angel, awake!*

I look up.

It's Jaime. I almost don't recognize her because her hair is straight and she's wearing beige: a minidress, embroidered with lobsters, that looks right on her somehow. She seems to have boiled off all her earlier incarnations— poufy-perm girl, slinky movie siren with a gardenia in her hair. Who knows? Maybe she'll burn through this one too.

"I thought I'd find you here," she says, and when she smiles, she is still Jaime.

"What brings you home?" I ask.

"Summer vacation," she says. There's a nervous catch in her voice, like she doesn't deserve something as frivolous as summer after what we've been through.

"They treating you well back there in . . . ?"

"New Hampshire? Well enough," she says. "Although

I'm notorious. The first time I didn't drink beer at a keg-ger, some wiseass said, 'You're *that* girl, aren't you?'"

I shake my head. "Sorry, Jay, I really am. But I still wouldn't have done anything differently."

"Me either," she's quick to say. "I'm glad we were there for him at the end. It's just that some days it's hard to find a way forward, you know? I'm not even sure I want to."

Wow. I'm not the only one holding on to the pain. This girl's just as twisted as me.

"Have you heard from Sonia?" she says.

I shrug. "She calls sometimes." It's true. You want to talk about guilt? There's a real case. She skipped town as soon as it was obvious that Evan wasn't getting any better and I would never replace him with someone else on bass. I suppose I shouldn't blame her. She told me up front she was only in it for the money. Every time I hear her voice over the phone and she talks about the weather in California, or the bands she's working with now, what she's really saying is *Forgive me for leaving.* And I do. Because I remember what it was like when you've done something so bad you'd give anything to put it behind you—even your left nostril.

There's something Sonia said during one call that puzzles me, though, and I decide Jay is the perfect per-son to ask about it.

I force a laugh. "Sonia says she doesn't remember Ziggy. Can you believe that? She's blanked on him com-pletely."

Jaime stares hard at me; her brow turns into a V shape like it used to when she was studying something. "I don't know what you're talking about."

I prompt her. "Ziggy? Our singer?"

"Noah," she says in a way that gets my attention. "You were Ziggy. You put on an English accent. Your singing voice dropped an octave. You led us. You acted so confident."

I figure if I stare enough, I'll understand what she's saying.

"We thought it was performance art. You know, like the real David Bowie? He put on these personas. We figured that was what you were doing. Channeling a real rock star that we could all get behind . . . I just thought you didn't know when to quit acting." She sees the expression on my face. "Oh. I see."

She can't be right. I don't understand. I saw him so clearly. The chicken fluff hair, the neatly pressed suits.

Wait a minute, did I ever see him clearly? Or was he always fuzzy around the edges?

I hear the truth of what she says, even if I don't feel it yet.

Jaime shakes her head. "I'm not surprised. You knew before any of us how sick Evan was."

I flash back to the night Ziggy first appeared. I always thought he showed himself because we'd lost my car. Then I remember Ev rolling on the sidewalk in pain. It wasn't the car that was lost, it was my best friend.

Jaime looks at her watch and mutters something about getting home. She came looking for me, but now she's sorry she did.

"I'll swing by again before I go. It's good seeing you, Noah."

After she's gone, I think about the band and how it took off after we played on the roof of Jojo's. We cut a record with a new label out of Seattle in the time between Evan's treatments. We never quite made it to arena-band status, but we sold out at every club we played. And it seemed the weaker Evan got, the more our fame spread.

I could never force myself to look at any of the memorabilia—the record itself, the posters, the articles—because it reminded me too much of the price we had to pay for our fame, and how long it took Evan to die.

But after what Jaime said about Ziggy, I know it's time to make myself look. Could she be right? Could I have been that deluded? Even before I pull our album from the "G" bin, I know what I'll find. I even begin to see how it might have happened.

For example: Say you're a punk-ass kid who's never known anything but glares and limited expectations, not to mention a "legacy of violence," as my shrink says.

Now say that your best friend is going through something horrible, and is about to go through something even worse, and you have to help him through it and you don't even get to keep him in the end. All you get to do is help him die. If you were me? You'd never have had the confidence to do what needed doing.

It would've been easier to believe in David Bowie.

My mind works a feedback loop around all the cryptic comments. *You don't need Ziggy. They're your words, man. You're the one with the talent. Wait a minute, help me understand: We're waiting for who?*

I feel like throwing up. It all falls into place. Like the Marr. Merciless. Springing out from hidden places, slowly and secretly taking over, eating people from the inside out. I can finally call it now what I couldn't call it then.

Cancer.

No way to do battle with it. Can't fight it head-on. You won't even have hope. Can only cocoon the victims in love, set them up high, and hope that there'll be moments when they transform into something more than a victim.

I lock the front door and hang a sign up. BACK IN 10. I go upstairs to my drafty apartment, pick up my Gibson Les Paul, and strum a few licks.

Could it be possible?

I try singing a few lines. I'm rusty at first, but then the old smoothness comes back into it. I feel that low range resonate in my skull. I can hear what I didn't understand.

Yes. Ziggy's voice is *my* voice. It may have sounded foreign last year, but now it sounds completely natural.

I pick up the phone. The first call I make lasts less than five minutes. Jaime is the second call.

"Hello?"

I have to search for the words. Then I remember: The words were always mine. "I just booked an acoustic set on Saturday at the Long Goodbye. I'd like you to come."

There's a pause on the other end.

I go on. "I know you're just here visiting. I know you have to go back to wherever . . ."

"New Hampshire."

"New Hampshire. It's just . . . I'd really like to see you."

There's another pause. This one I don't try to fill. She is thinking and I can hear it over the phone, in the way she breathes.

She sighs. "Noah, I don't know what you're asking . . ."

I brace myself for rejection.

". . . but I'll be there."

The pause is all on my end of the phone now.

Jaime goes on. "I know we haven't seen each other in a while, but I've lost so much . . . I know what's important. You're important. And talented. I can't wait to hear you sing again."

And she hangs up without saying good-bye.

I try to dampen my mood. Maybe it's not what I think. Maybe we won't carve out safe spaces in the dark, run our hands through each other's hair while around us neon lights sizzle. Maybe it's not even worth trying, because Evan still looms large between us. Or maybe it's *because* Evan looms so large between us that I want to hold on to her.

It's too late for me to worry about any of that, because I'm a musician. I hear things that aren't there. And slowly, they're arranging themselves into possibilities.

I pick up my guitar. Never mind how much time I've lost.

I'm finally ready to begin.

ACKNOWLEDGMENTS

In December 1984 I came home to Gresham, Oregon, from my first semester of college. My parents had kept my memorabilia from high school in a corner in the basement—things I had collected that had no value to anyone but me. There were buttons from Django's Records I'd bought for a dollar apiece that had slogans on them. *The Moral Majority Is Neither. My Karma Ran Over My Dogma.* And tacked to a piece of decaying cork, a poster my friends and I had ripped from a telephone pole. It was printed on orange paper, was in pristine condition, and read, *Billy Rancher and the Unreal Gods Wake the Dead.*

It took me a long time to realize my prize piece of memorabilia was now morbid.

A lot of things had changed in the three months since I'd been in Portlandia, and one of them was that Billy Rancher, the darling of Portland's rock scene, was slowly, and publicly, dying from lymphoma. He was twenty-nine when he died in 1986, and he kept performing up to the end.

If you believed the newspapers and rock critics at the time, the whole city adored him and was his friend. But looking back, I can't help wishing that, in those final months of his life, Billy Rancher had had at least one really good friend, like Noah, who would have given up anything for him—even knowing that he'd have to let him go.

The Rise & Fall of the Gallivanters was a difficult book to write, and I'm grateful that I'm surrounded by people of Noah's generosity and magnitude. My first and best reader, Peggy King Anderson, for example. And Steven Chudney of the Chudney Agency, who, when I said, "I'm worried about placing this one. It's weird," replied, "I *loved* it."

A giant thank-you to Maggie Lehrman at Abrams, who also appreciated weird, then Tamar Brazis and Orlando Dos Reis, who made the unimaginable parts blend more smoothly into the narrative.

And finally, I couldn't have made it through such a difficult process if not for my family, Juan, Sofia, and Ricky. Juan for putting up with me in general, and Sofia and Ricky for letting me hug them when I have a bad day, even though they're too old for it to be cool.

Go do some gallivanting of your own, kiddos. I've got your back.